ELVIS FINDS A BONE

RECKLESS CAMPER COZY MYSTERY SERIES
BOOK FOUR

LIBBY HOWARD

LIBBY HOWARD
WHODUNNITS WITH HEART

CHAPTER 1

*R*eckless Neighbors App:
    The Reckless Sniffers Club will be holding a field scent detection event this Saturday. Come out, cheer on our tracking dogs, and enjoy free donuts and coffee! Call Mike Allen for more information about the event or about joining our club.

I adjusted the bright red harness around Elvis's chest, snapping the forty-foot lead to the ring at the top. The hound was alert and excited, his head high, his ears forward, his tail curved into a long "C" over his rear. It had been over two years since we'd done an organized tracking event together, almost a year since the last time I'd attended a Search and Rescue Group meeting. My cancer treatment had put those kinds of activities on hold, and so had my purchase of Reckless Camper Campground, but I'd seen a notice on our neighborhood app from the local tracking club, and decided it was time to return to our hobby. One quick online application and an internet payment later, and I was now a member of the Reckless Sniffers.

This was Elvis's and my first event, our first time even meeting the other club members. I was a little nervous, and had already downed two chocolate frosted donuts and a large coffee from the food table in a futile attempt to calm my nerves.

"No pressure, buddy," I told Elvis, who ignored me.

My hound had been one of the stars of our former tracking club. He had a great nose, and unbreakable focus when on the trail, usually heading straight to the correct item and sitting to indicate he'd reached the tracking object. Seventy percent of the time, he'd scored in the top three of our group at scent detection events.

But the other thirty percent...

Sometimes Elvis arbitrarily decided to track a scent that wasn't the one I'd set him on. In those cases I'd found myself staring down at the wrapper from a discarded chicken sandwich, or some spilled potato chips, or cookie crumbs—all of which Elvis would hoover into his mouth. The hound loved tracking, but he also loved eating. Sometimes a chicken sandwich took precedence over a tracking scent, and I couldn't exactly blame Elvis for that. I liked a good chicken sandwich myself.

He'd done much better at search and rescue, happier finding people and animals than determining which container had clove as opposed to the seven boxes with other scents. By the time I'd had to quit, Elvis had been close to testing for his SARs certification, but I was sure we'd need to relearn a lot of things we'd both forgotten.

Today was supposed to be a friendly competition, but looking around, I could see these people took their tracking seriously.

"You the new member?" A man in his midsixties who was wearing an honest-to-God tweed jacket with a matching hat put out his hand. "I'm Andy Treeling. And this here is Xanadu."

"Sassy Letouroux." I shook his hand. "And this is Elvis."

Xanadu was a white foxhound with a lean, athletic body and big tan and black spots. Her tail wagged slowly as she and Elvis touched noses, then each went to sniff the other's caboose sections.

"Good looking bloodhound," Andy said with a nod toward Elvis. "Have you met Marcus LaSalle? He's got a bloodhound as well. Bought him for dog shows, but after a few years and no wins, he decided he'd do tracking instead. Dog's got like six names, none of which make any darned sense, so we just call him 'Nose.'"

I glanced around and saw a tall, dark-haired man with a black-and-tan bloodhound. "He's gorgeous," I said, meaning the dog, not the guy. The man was attractive, but the hound was definitely the looker of the pair. "I'm guessing Nose is the dog to beat today?"

"Nose is good, but he's not the real competition. Ellen Preston's Lab, Harper, is a strong contender, but the winning dog is usually Marcie Boarding's Sarge."

There were four other women here besides me. One was Ellen Preston, the forty-something blonde with her yellow Labrador Retriever, the second was a middle-aged woman of color with a German Wirehair Pointer, the third a twenty-something Southeast Asian woman with a French Bulldog, and the fourth a woman that looked to be my age with her snow-white hair pulled back into a messy bun. At her side, attentive and focused, was a Doberman.

"Is Sarge the pointer?" I asked. "Or the Dobie?"

Sarge wasn't exactly an uncommon name for a dog, but if I were to make a guess, I'd say this particular Sarge was the Doberman. They were fast, smart, obedient dogs, and it wouldn't surprise me one bit that a Dobie would excel at scent detection. But pointers were no slouch either when it came to nose work.

"The Dobie," Andy told me. "Pauline's pointer, Thor, is

good, but he's new to tracking and still not much more than a puppy. Give him a couple years and he'll probably be leaving us all in the dust."

I nodded, then looked again at the Asian woman with the French Bulldog. *Which one of these things, is not like the others...*

"What's the story with the Frenchie?" I didn't want to diss anyone's dog, but French Bulldogs had adorably smushed snouts that didn't really lend themselves to nose work. And as enthusiastic and energetic as they were, those stubby little legs would lose time compared to the larger dogs.

"Jessica's our social director, so she always brings the coffee and donuts." Andy nodded toward the food-and-drink table. "Actually Curly is kind of our club mascot. We give him a breed and size handicap and with the adjustments he usually scores pretty well. Plus he's so darned cute."

Curly *was* cute. I was a sucker for any dog, but the bouncy little white bulldog inspired an urge in me to scratch his head and tell him what a good boy he was. Although all the dogs here were beautiful in their own distinctive way. I looked around at the other members, and noticed something. Every dog except for Elvis had a strange, orange-colored collar with a coated wire antennae sticking a good foot out the side.

I leaned forward and pointed at the one Xanadu wore. "Is this a club thing? Should I have bought one of these before I came to an event?"

"No, it's not required that you have one. They're GPS collars." Andy showed me something that looked like a small television remote. "They run on satellite and on cell service. Most of us use our dogs for hunting, and this allows us to find them if they get out of visual range."

That was amazing and something I really needed to think about getting for Elvis. "Does it have a vibration button?

Sometimes I use an e-collar on Elvis when he's on the scent and his ears are turned off."

Andy laughed. "I totally understand. Xanadu is the same when she's got her nose to the ground. These only have the GPS locator, but I think there are models with a vibration function. Ask Mike. He's some big-time executive for Rio Grande Electronics. Got the club members all a discount on these last year, so he might be able to get you a discount as well."

Mike Allen was the president of the club, and the man I'd spoken to when I was making inquiries about Elvis and me joining. I looked around, spotting the bald man over near the coffee and donut table.

"I'll definitely talk to him," I told Andy. I liked to make as many of my purchases locally as I could, and tried to keep to small businesses, but online shopping was convenient, and Rio Grande Electronics was the most convenient of all with their same-day shipping and two-day delivery guarantees.

"How do you think Elvis will do today?" Andy asked.

I shrugged, because this was a scent detection event and not a SAR one. We'd be looking for little tins in the tall grass of the field that contained the matching essential oil to the target scent in the jar we randomly picked. It was a roll of the dice whether Elvis would remember his training, or even think the scent I'd chosen was worth the bother of tracking.

But I needed to be positive.

"I'm hoping he can beat the Lab. And maybe the Dobie as well," I said, my competitive spirit surging. I tried to tamp it down with the rationalization that it had been quite a while since Elvis and I had done this. I didn't want to set unrealistic expectations for today. If Elvis didn't end up following a trail to someone's leftover lunch, I'd consider it a win.

Besides that, there were reasons Sarge and Harper might outperform two bloodhounds who had tracking and nose-work bred into their DNA. First, trainability. Second, versatility.

Bloodhounds excelled at tracking people and animals. Scent hounds didn't just have great noses, they had the independence, the drive and focus, and the persistence to keep searching for a lost scent long after other breeds might have given up.

But while other breeds may not quite have a hound's nose ability, they were often able to switch things up and track spices, drugs, or anything else. Bloodhounds tended to pick favorites and be uninterested in tracking other scents. I'd long been a fan of Labradors with their quick ability to learn and their easygoing nature. And Dobermans as well, with their intelligence, strong chase-drive, incredible loyalty, and the determination that meant they didn't give up easily either.

Elvis? He was focused, independent, and stubborn. But his recall was hit or miss, especially when he was on a scent. It had taken him five times as long to learn a task compared to others in his obedience classes, not because he wasn't smart. He just wasn't interested. Why sit and stay when there was an intriguing smell over there? Why bother jumping over an obstacle when there were scents to inhale? And why come when called? Didn't his human understand the priority was always in sniffing, in finding, not in racing over at her beck and call?

Put a well-trained bloodhound on a two-week cold trail after three days of rain and he'd find that lost kid in the forest. But here, at this event? Who knew how well, or poorly, we'd do.

"Ooo, we're getting ready to start." Andy pointed to Mike Allen, who was gesturing to gather everyone near. "Good luck to you and Elvis."

"And good luck to you and Xanadu," I replied.

We each were to go one-at-a-time, selecting one of several glass jars that looked like they should have been used to can jelly. Inside the jar was a scent-laced cotton ball. Our dog was to sniff the odor inside the jar, then start tracking, eventually—hopefully—leading their handler to the metal tin with a matching-scented cotton ball that was hidden some-where in the tall grasses of this field.

It wasn't nearly as easy as it sounded. We had drawn numbers that signified the order in which we'd search, and those who went first would have a relatively clear field in which to track. Those at the end? Their dog had to sort through the smells of all the competing dogs and their handlers who'd zig-zagged across the same terrain, possibly messing up the scent trails. The metal tins were perforated with holes to ensure the scent wafted out, but today's lack of wind meant that the dogs wouldn't have a scent-cone to catch and follow back to the target item. They'd need to search on a grid pattern and hope they were quick in finding the matching tin.

There were eight competitors. I'd drawn number eight. And Elvis had been out of work for two years. Yes, he'd tracked down several deceased bodies in the past few months, but I hadn't set him out to find those bodies, and he wasn't trained to do cadaver work, so none of that counted.

We led our dogs over to the table filled with carafes of coffee and boxes of donuts. Mike went over the rules and the process for the event, then we got started. The Dobie went first, sniffing the contents of the jar at his owner's command, then sitting at attention, ears upright and dark eyes fixed on his human.

"Find," Marcie told the dog. Sarge took off like a shot.

The Doberman was unleashed, and I had a twinge of envy at the woman's confidence in her recall. The tall weeds of the field vibrated as Sarge crashed through them. Marcie followed, holding back and to the side so she didn't accidently cross the scent trail. Outside of the noise Sarge made crushing foliage under paw, he was silent and focused, his nose firmly to the ground. He was tall enough that I could see the dark line of his back and the stub of his tail over the patches of weeds—an advantage for us spectators while watching him work.

I could clearly see the dog's methodical search pattern, as well as the moment when he'd locked onto the scent. It was like Moses parting the Red Sea as the Doberman tore through the weeds, Marcie following as quickly as the footing would allow. Suddenly the dog halted and sat, his noble head like a statue of Anubis as it appeared above the green and gold vegetation.

"Hold your dog," Mike called out. His instruction was unnecessary as the obedient Sarge was frozen in place. Marcie reached him first, but remained a few feet behind the dog until Mike caught up.

The man bent down and came up with a metal bucket. Sarge's eyes followed the bucket, but the rest of him remained unmoving. The club president removed a metal tin and looked at the number on the bottom.

"I'm sorry, but this is the incorrect scent," Mike announced.

Marcie made a choked, incredulous noise, her mouth open. The rest of us sucked in a breath, equally amazed. So much for the ringer of this event. Sarge had failed to bring home the trophy, and I got the impression that was a rare occurrence.

Every dog had his bad days. Either Sarge was a little off, or this supposedly friendly event was far more challenging than I'd anticipated.

Or there had been a mistake.

Marcie clearly was going with option three.

"That's impossible," the woman sputtered. "It's sweet birch. I clearly smelled it when I showed Sarge the jar. The target scent was sweet birch. Someone put the wrong number on that tin."

"I put the scents in the tins and in the jars, and I put the number on myself." Mike scowled. "And it's not sweet birch in this tin."

"Then Sarge locked onto a secondary scent," Marcie insisted. "If you put the sweet birch in the initial jar and something else in this tin, he was probably following your scent instead of the animal's one."

I considered that a second. In prior events I'd been to, the same person loaded the target and tracking boxes and also put them into the field, just to avoid this very thing. Plus most scent dogs were trained to track specific scents and not humans. It was mainly the Search and Rescue programs whose dogs could make this mistake since those dogs were primarily trained to follow human scents.

Some events were SARs focused. Others were focused on animal scents, appealing to those who trained their dogs in game retrieval. More commonly the events used spices and other strong oils in tracking. Dogs trained in one kind of event were at a bit of a disadvantage when it came to the others

"I used disposable gloves when I applied the oil to each scent pair. And I used tongs to place the buckets and tins. I was the only one handling and placing the scent containers," Mike told the woman.

"Well, maybe the oils from the sweet birch jar somehow got on your hand or the other gloves when you loaded this tin," Marcie argued.

Mike scowled at the accusation that he'd been careless. After a deep breath, he made visible effort to calm himself.

"Sarge is a talented tracking dog, and one of the best in

9

the Reckless Sniffers Club, but maybe you need to spend some extra time working on the different scents with him," Mike snapped.

Those were clearly fighting words. Marcie reached out for the tin and threw it on the ground. She and Mike stepped into each other voices raised and fingers jabbing into each other as they argued.

Sarge had been watching the exchange, only his eyes moving back and forth between the two humans. At this point he rose from his sit, his lips curled back in a snarl. I caught my breath, worried that the dog would intervene and defend his human. I didn't want to think what the sleek dog could do to Mike, or the repercussions of even a minor bite. The pair would be kicked out of the club, Marcie could be fined, and Sarge might even lose his life.

Before the Doberman could act, a long mournful bay filled the air. I looked down at the hound by my side. There was Elvis, his head lifted to the sky, his loud, deep baritone practically shaking the ground.

Nose, the other bloodhound, responded in kind, followed by a higher-timber cry of the foxhound and even higher yip of the French bulldog. In less than a second, every dog at the event aside from the Dobie was vocal.

The noise disrupted the argument between Mike and Marcie. Both turned to see what the commotion was about. Sarge's snarl faded and he sat once more, looking at the other dogs with an expression of curiosity on his sculpted face.

I wasn't sure what Mike and Marcie said to each other at that point, but I was guessing they agreed to discuss this later, when the event was over and when they'd both had time to calmly assess the situation.

The rest of the event went smoothly, but as Mike examined each tin it became clear that Elvis and I were in over our heads. My hound was good at differentiating animal scents, and even better at tracking humans, but these were scent oils used in AKC and other regulation events. We weren't all that skilled at this sort of scent detection. Plus the lack of a breeze, the tall grasses, and the buckets that held and blocked the scent emanating from the perforated tins were clearly making this a very difficult task for even the most experienced of tracking dogs.

The cotton balls had been spiked with a drop of sweet birch, anise, clove, cypress, vetiver, pine, wintergreen, or myrrh. I wasn't sure Elvis would be at all interested in most of those scents. The novelty might intrigue him, or he could decide that he'd rather find a pile of deer poop rather than the scent I'd asked him to locate. But I decided I wasn't going to worry about any of that. We were here to have fun, to reintroduce ourselves to tracking, and to meet others in the local tracking club. If the perfect Sarge had failed to locate the correct box, then I wasn't going to sweat if Elvis also failed today.

I repeated that to myself like a mantra, but truthfully I was more than a little competitive when it came to these things. I'd learned early on to curb that competition when winning relied pretty much on my sometimes unpredictable bloodhound, but deep down I still wanted to win. There might not be a trophy or even a certificate for today's event, but I wanted this new club to see that Elvis wasn't just a pretty boy with a nose, that he was a dog who could really track a scent.

Out of the seven other competing dogs, only two had managed to find the correct box. The dogs to beat right now were the yellow Lab, Harper, and her human, Ellen Preston, and, surprisingly, the little French Bulldog, Curly.

Ellen had gone second and I would be going last, so we'd chatted off to the side as I waited my turn. I really took a liking to her. She'd grown up in a dog show family, but had taken to obedience trials and Fast-cat competitions when she'd been in her teens. At thirty, she'd discovered tracking and that had been her main focus ever since. As a pup, Harper had excelled in obedience, eventually earning her championship there. She'd also brought home quite a few ribbons in the Fast CAT racing competitions, but she really enjoyed scent work. Harper had both the nose and the dedication to really shine as a tracking dog, and Ellen was equally enthusiastic about the sport.

By the time Elvis and I stepped up to receive our jar with the target scent, my fantasies of winning had suffered a reality check. Elvis still had a shot, but Harper's score would be hard to beat. Honestly it would be hard to beat Curly's handicapped score. Even Thor, the German Wirehair Pointer's, and Xanadu, Andy's dog, had performed well today, although none of them had been able to locate the correct scent tin.

I opened the jar, eyeing the cotton ball inside before lowering the jar down for Elvis to sniff.

"Work," I told him, even though he was already smelling the contents of the jar. If you put anything in front of a canine nose, they'd sniff it, but a bloodhound in particular saw the world through smell. Still, I wanted Elvis to know that he'd be expected to locate whatever was inside, and not just enjoy a good smelling opportunity.

I let the hound take a good long sniff since the timer didn't start until I set the dog off.

"Ready?" I asked.

Reluctantly pulling his nose from the box, Elvis looked up at me. His dark droopy eyes sparkled with anticipation. His tongue lolled from the heavy folds of his mouth. His long thick tail swept slowly back and forth.

"Find," I told him.

I didn't need to ask the hound twice. Elvis took off at the

word with a speed that belied the stereotypes of a lazy bloodhound. I gripped the red leash, letting it out as he ran. I was the last entry of the day, so it wasn't all that important for me to hold back or stay off to the side. I wouldn't be messing up anyone else's scent trail, and any damage I might do to my own had probably been done by the seven competitors that came before me.

Elvis was hauling butt through the field, trampling grasses with his nose firmly rooted to the ground. I hurried after him, trying to stay out of his way and feeling a little guilty that I'd ever doubted my dog. I'd never seen him this focused, this driven. Maybe the time off tracking had been good for him. Maybe he'd matured over the last year and could focus more on the task at hand. Maybe whatever scent was in that jar was something that really, really interested Elvis. Either way, he was moving at a pace that made me think we might have a chance at beating Harper and Ellen Preston after all.

With a sudden burst of speed, Elvis took off. I let out the remaining slack in the leash, racing after him as fast as I could. The hound made a sudden left and I frowned, wondering if Mike had actually put the boxes this far toward the edge of the field. But I needed to trust in my hound, so I pivoted, stumbling as I tried to keep up with Elvis.

Elvis kept running, straining against the leash with his hundred pounds of muscle. We were heading for the woods, and I was pretty sure that wasn't where any of the tins had been placed, but I just didn't have the strength to reel Elvis in. I barely had the strength to hold onto the leash.

"Off course," Mike yelled.

I dug in my heels and leaned backward, trying to stop the hound's momentum, but he kept going and I was jerked forward. I threw out my hands and they hit the ground before the rest of me. The leash flew free. Scrambling to my knees and onto my feet I yelled for my dog, knowing how futile my calls were. When he was on a scent, his ears seemed to turn off. The only thing that ever broke his concentration and brought him back to me was the vibration collar—the one I'd left at home because it would be too embarrassing to admit that I had a dog whose voice recall was iffy at best.

Not as embarrassing as having my dog run off in the middle of an event, though.

I raced for the woods where Elvis had disappeared. Hearing something that sounded like a herd of elephants crashing through the weeds, I glanced back and saw that Mike and the other participants were hurrying my way.

Great. Not only had I lost my dog, but I now had most of the Reckless Sniffers Club coming to help me look for him. So much for all that SARs training Elvis and I had done. What had he been tracking, running off into the woods like that? He'd been hot of the trail of something, but whatever it was, it wasn't the scent that was in the tin.

I stopped at the treeline, still calling Elvis's name. Mortified as I was, I was also worried for my hound. It was probably a good thing I'd have these other people helping me look for him. Maybe we could put the other tracking dogs to work. If Sarge couldn't find Elvis, I was willing to bet that yellow Lab, Harper, could.

The others caught up, all of them breathing heavy from their race through the field.

"Do you have a GPS collar on him?" Mike asked me.

"No." That was absolutely something I needed to purchase. "He's microchipped," I added, thinking that at least if someone found him and turned him in to the pound, I'd be notified.

Animal Control was the least of my worries though. Elvis on the scent was liable to run right in front of a speeding truck. Or he could encounter a not-so-friendly farmer who might shoot him. Or someone could decide to keep him, chained up in the backyard for the rest of his life.

I took a deep breath and slowly let it out, trying to calm myself down. He was going to be fine. We just needed to organize a search party, complete with tracking dogs, and find my hound.

"What was in that tin?" I asked Mike, wondering what Elvis was *supposed* to be tracking.

"Pine," Mike told me.

I groaned. Elvis had been trained to detect the scent of pine. That should have been an easy job for him. We should have found the tin in record time, beating even Harper. But noooo. My hound had evidently found something more interesting to track.

"Why don't Andy, Marcie, and Ellen take that side of the woods," Mike directed. "Marcus…"

Mike's voice trailed off, and I turned to see what had caused the stunned expression on his face.

It was Elvis, coming out of the woods, trailing a red forty-foot leash behind him. In his mouth was a giant bone—a bone with a dirty hiking boot attached to one end.

CHAPTER 2

"*E*lvis was supposed to locate a tin with pine in it," I told Jake. "The scent of pine, that is. It's not like there was actually a pine tree in that box, just some random cotton ball with a little pine-scent oil on it."

"This is a bone and not a pine-scented cotton ball," Sean commented.

"Sure is. Don't know any pine-scented cotton balls that wear size thirteen hiking boots either," Jake added.

"This is definitely not a pine-scented cotton ball, in my expert opinion," Stef announced.

The dry humor from our deputies and the coroner *was* a little funny, but my hound had still found a body somewhere in the woods and brought home a leg. With a foot. With a boot still on it. Which was way creepier than it was funny.

"Elvis sure does seem to like tracking people," Sean said. "You said he was SARs trained?"

"Yes, we were working to be part of a search and rescue group a few years ago, but he was never trained as a cadaver dog," I replied.

Dogs who found deceased people were specially taught,

and I'd never done that with Elvis. Clearly the last few months had shown me that he was good at it, but as important as that specialty was, I'd only wanted the two of us to track live people.

"Well, this is obviously a human leg bone," Stef announced. "It's pretty clean, so I'm guessing the man was in a shallow grave, if he was in a grave at all. I might be able to get some DNA off the foot or the inside of the shoe. Hopefully there is DNA on file with a missing person's report and we'll be able to get a match."

"And give a family closure," Jake added soberly. "We don't have that many hikers that go missing around here, but lots of people use these trails as part of a months-long backpacking trip, so we should check missing persons reports up and down the Eastern states, just in case."

"I should be able to narrow down a range for the time of death once I do some lab work, but just eyeballing this bone, I'd say he was out there for around a year. Not more than two though, I'm guessing."

Jake turned to me. "Any chance there's more than the leg out there?"

I glanced toward the forest. "Well, I'm pretty sure the rest of him is *somewhere*, but whether it's where the Elvis found the leg or not, I don't know. He yanked the leash out of my hand and took off into the woods. Before we could go look for him, he was back with the leg in his mouth."

"Scavengers can spread bones over a pretty wide area," Stef commented. "Jake, why don't you and Sassy see if Elvis can lead you back to where he found this. Call me if you find anything. If this is all Elvis is able to find, we'll need to get a few cadaver dogs in here to search. I really want the rest of this man located."

Not only would it help her cause-of-death determination, but the family would want to bury all of this man's remains, not just his leg. Plus, no one wanted hikers or hunters stumbling on the other leg, or other bones. There was no sense in anyone besides me and the Reckless Sniffers Club members having that unnerving experience.

"Do you think Elvis can take us to where he found the bone?" Jake asked me.

I nodded and after a second of thought, handed him the leash. "He's pretty strong when he's on a scent trail, and I don't want to lose him again."

It was embarrassing admitting that I wasn't strong enough to hold my own dog back, or that my dog wouldn't listen to my recall, but it was the truth. I definitely needed to get one of those GPS collars for Elvis. And next time, I was putting aside my pride and making him wear the vibration collar as well. The poor dog was going to have collars layered up half his neck, but at least I wouldn't lose him in the vast expanse of woods that made up the park system.

"He'll need to sniff the leg again," I warned Stef.

She grimaced. "Just make sure he doesn't gnaw on it, or take off with it, or anything."

"He won't." It was a promise I couldn't guarantee Elvis would keep, but in spite of the disaster of the day, I had to have some faith in my hound's training.

"Work," I told the dog. His ears pricked forward and he stood, tail wagging.

Once he was focused on me, I bent down and pointed to the leg, trying to get close enough so there would be no misunderstanding, but far enough that I wasn't actually touching the thing.

"Work," I repeated.

Elvis bent down, snuffling loudly as he ran his nose up and down the leg, spending a little extra time on the shoe. When I thought he'd gotten enough scent, I told him to "Find."

Jake braced his feet, gripping the leash tight, but Elvis just looked up at me, sat, then looked back down at the bone.

"Maybe that's all there was," Sean suggested.

"He still should track the scent back to the original site." I sighed, pointing once more to the leg. "Work."

Please lead us back where you found it, Elvis, I pleaded silently. *Please be a good boy and show everyone what an amazing tracking dog you are. Please.*

"Find," I told the hound, crossing my fingers behind my back. "Find."

Elvis looked up at me, his brow wrinkled, then, much to my relief, he dropped his nose to the ground and started tracking.

I knew, a few minutes in, that something was wrong. We weren't following the path we'd taken when I'd brought him back from the woods, the bone still in his mouth. We weren't even heading toward the woods. Instead, Elvis zig-zagged around the field, coming to a stop and sitting in front of a small bucket.

I sighed, picking it up and taking the metal tin out. Turning it over, I read the number on the back.

"Five," I said.

"That's not the correct tin," Mike informed me. He and the entire club had stayed, curious about the bone and what the police would say. "The correct tin was number two, with the pine scent. This is cypress."

Pine and cypress smelled the same to me. Elvis's nose was far more sensitive, but there had to be some similarities between the two. A good scent detection dog should have been able to easily differentiate the two smells, but I knew that Elvis occasionally got lazy when it came to this kind of tracking. He'd probably figured an evergreen was an evergreen. Close enough, in his opinion.

Either way, I clearly had a lot of remedial training to do

with the hound before he'd recover his obviously lost former skills.

"Not that it matters," Mike went on. "You were disqualified once he went off course the first time."

"Are you sure he's a tracking dog?" Marcie taunted, not even bothering to hide her smile.

Jerk. Especially coming from someone's who star-quality dog hadn't managed to find the correct tin either.

"Find," I repeated, a note of desperation in my voice.

I blew out a breath as Elvis once more dropped his nose, this time heading in a fast trot toward the woods. Jake and I ran after him, Sean close behind us. The rest of the tracking club followed at a respectable distance, not wanting to intrude what was clearly a police matter, but too curious to stay behind.

Elvis took us on a winding path through saplings, brambles, and a thick cover of leaves that hadn't quite decomposed from last fall. About three hundred feet into the woods, he stopped in a grove of old-growth pine and sat.

The area with its carpet of brown and orange needles had been stirred up—probably by Elvis when he'd retrieved the leg bone, but I wasn't ruling out other animal traffic. This was the perfect spot for deer to bed down in, and these woods were also home to squirrels, raccoons, bear, and other wildlife.

And the fact that it was a pine grove didn't escape me. Maybe Elvis caught the scent of these trees from the field and had decided a pine was a pine.

Jake and I stayed slightly out of the clearing, waiting for the others to catch up. Elvis must have decided that our inaction meant he was released from his sit. The hound rose, and instead of coming back to me, he started to dig.

"No!" Jake and I both yelled at the same time.

Elvis hesitated, but then got back to task.

"Elvis, come. Free. Leave it," I continued shouting, hoping one of those commands would stop my hound.

I wanted to jump into the clearing and stop my dog, but I also didn't want to further disturb what might be a crime scene. Although my footprints probably wouldn't do near the damage of Elvis's digging.

Jake did not hesitate. Still gripping the leash, he ran into the clearing and grabbed Elvis by his harness, hauling him up and away from where he was digging. With a few firm words and his hand still holding the dog's harness, he led a chastised Elvis back to where I stood. I took over from there, making Elvis sit by my side and tying the long leash to a nearby tree trunk, just in case the hound tried to make a break for it.

"You're a *good* boy." I gave the dog's chest a quick scratch as I reassured him. Yes, he'd bolted away from me during a tracking event, failing to find the scent I'd sent him after. Yes, it had taken a few tries for him to lead us back to this clearing. And yes, he'd been digging when all his training had told him that was *not* what he should do when he'd reached the end of his trail. But in spite of all that, he'd found a body. Scary/creepy as that was, it was a good thing he'd found it. From what the coroner had said, this man's remains had been in the woods for a year or more. His family deserved closure. And no one should have their final resting place undiscovered in a forest, their friends and family not knowing what happened to them.

"Is this...did you find the rest of him?" Sean asked as he carefully picked his way around the edge of the clearing closer to where Jake stood.

"I don't know if it's all of him, but there are clearly additional bones here." Jake pointed to where Elvis had been digging. "And they look human to me, but we'll need to get Stef to confirm that."

Sean pulled a phone from his pocket. "I'll call her. Might need to walk out a bit to get a cell signal, though. Kinda sketchy with the heavy tree cover here."

It was one of the problems living in the verdant mountains of Virginia. Thick canopies of tree leaves made for a very patchy cell signal and lots of dead spots.

Sean stepped away down the trail, holding his phone aloft and staring at the screen. The members of the Reckless Sniffers Club had arrived as well and were gathered behind me, straining to see if they could catch a glimpse of whatever Jake had seen in the clearing.

"I wonder who it is," Ellen Preston whispered. "We're a couple miles from the popular trails. I can't imagine a hiker bushwhacking around this part of the park lands."

"That might have been the problem," Marcus told her. "People go off trail to pee or find level ground to set up camp, then they get turned around. That happened to some woman on the AT years ago. She wandered completely off-trail. Ended up dying."

"Someone died this year on the AT, too," Andy added. "I don't think they were lost, but they succumbed to exposure."

The more recent tragic death on the Appalachian Trail that Andy referred to had been in New Hampshire, but we had winter hikers here in Virginia, and could have some unexpectedly severe weather in the mountains. It wasn't out of the realm of possibility that the man had died of exposure, so close to shelter and help.

It also wasn't out of the realm of possibility that this was a suicide. I hated to think that, but too many people walked into the woods each year with no intention of returning.

"Even if exposure doesn't kill them, sometimes starvation does," the man who owned the German Shepherd chimed in. "Backpackers can only carry so much food."

"It takes weeks to starve to death though," Pauline, who

owned Thor the German Wirehair Pointer, countered. "I don't think a starvation death would happen here like it does in Alaska or out west. I mean, even deep in the forest, you're still only a few days hike from *some* kind of town, or at least some person's farm."

"Unless people spend days getting delirious and wandering in circles," the German Shepherd owner argued. "He could have had a medical emergency though. A heart attack, or a stroke. Or he had a seizure or some sort of diabetic incident."

"Or dehydration," Jessica, the woman with the Frenchie, chimed in. "A family and their dog died of dehydration hiking out west a few years back."

Marcus snorted. "There's water everywhere here on the east coast. You can't go half a mile without there being a stream or creek or something. It's not like he was hiking in the Sierra Nevadas. Even without a filter, the guy should have been able to drink enough water to get to civilization before some bacteria took him down."

"I don't see a backpack, though." Ellen stood on her tip-toes as she looked into the clearing. "Maybe he wasn't a hiker. Maybe someone killed him and buried him in a shallow grave. Otherwise wouldn't he be laying on top of the ground with all his gear on or near him?"

"Stef Ostlund said he died around a year ago," Andy said. "So there could have been all sorts of pine needles, leaves, dirt, and stuff that fell on his remains over the months. And maybe he ditched his pack when he got desperate. Or he was an unprepared day-hiker."

The others murmured in agreement, but I wasn't convinced. Elvis had been *digging*. This wasn't just a lump of a body covered with dried pine needles. Whoever this was, I was beginning to think someone *had* buried them. And there was no reason for a person to dig a shallow grave for a hiker they'd come across that had died of exposure, and never report it. I wasn't a hundred percent convinced, but I was starting to think the person had been murdered and buried here. It explained the lack of any backpacking gear and Elvis needing to dig for the rest of his remains.

The sound of footsteps crunching through the forest silenced us all and we watched as Sean returned, leading Stef Ostlund and one of her techs. Sean and the tech held back while Stef walked up to where Jake stood.

"Did you start to dig him up?" she asked the sometimes-deputy.

Jake shook his head. "Elvis did. I grabbed him and pulled him off—hopefully before he disturbed too much of the scene."

Stef knelt down, brushing dirt away with a gloved hand and revealing a glimpse of white bone and what looked like torn, dirty fabric.

"Bullet hole. In his skull." She pointed as she said the words. "Pretty sure I can confidently say that's the cause of death, but let's see if the rest of this poor man can tell us more."

The club and I collectively sucked in a breath. Stef's meaning was clear.

The man whose grave Elvis had uncovered had most likely been murdered.

CHAPTER 3

"So, did our handsome boy bring home the gold?" Mom asked as she ruffled Elvis's ears and fed him one of the dog biscuits she kept on a shelf behind the register.

"No, he brought home a leg bone. With a foot. And a hiking boot still attached." I paused to let that sink in. "Yes, once again, Elvis has found a dead body."

"Oh no. Not again." Mom frowned. "A leg? What about the rest of the body?"

"Oh, we eventually got him to go back to where he found the leg to unearth the rest of the body, but it took a while. Jake and Sean were with us that time, though, so it wasn't quite as disturbing as having Elvis appear out of the woods with a leg bone in his mouth."

"Ugh!" Lottie threw her hands into the air. "You *always* find the bodies when I'm not around."

"That's not true," I countered. "You were there for the body in Danielle's field. Even if you weren't by my side the second I saw it, you were only a hundred feet away at most, and you saw it within minutes of my finding it."

I'd texted Lottie as soon as Elvis and I had left the tracking event, telling her to meet me at the camp store since I knew she'd want to hear this story in person. She beat me there and had been sitting at the little café table with mom, both of them drinking coffees when Elvis and I had arrived.

"Not good enough," Lottie complained. "One out of four bodies? That's inexcusable. From now on, I'm spending every waking minute with you, Sassy. Be prepared for me to be camped out in front of your house every night as well as being your creepy neighbor stalker while you go about your day. I absolutely refuse to miss out on the next murder victim you discover."

"Be prepared for some very boring days ahead," I warned her. Not that Lottie was serious. I *was* sure that my friend and neighbor was bummed about missing this latest discovery of Elvis and mine, but her fear of missing out wasn't enough to make her really camp out in front of my house every night.

At least I hoped not.

I told the pair of them the details of the tracking event, including Elvis running off into the woods and his reappearance with the bone.

"Was the man actually *murdered*?" Mom asked. "Maybe he was a hiker that died from exposure? Someone died on the AT this year, you know. They got caught in an unexpected late-spring snow storm without adequate clothing or shelter."

"That's what we all were thinking, but Elvis had to *dig* to expose the bones," I pointed out. "I figured that meant someone buried him. Then when Stef said there was a bullet hole in the man's head, our theories of a lost hiker went right out the window."

"Murder." Lottie grimaced. "I wonder if he was shot there in the woods, or shot elsewhere and moved to the woods for burial? It sounds horrible, but there have been hunting accidents before. The ones I've heard of weren't fatal, were always reported, and clearly accidents, but maybe a hunter was impaired or careless, and he panicked. Rather than call for an ambulance or the police, he buried the victim and just hoped no one ever found him."

I stared at her, aghast. "Lottie, that's horrible."

Any murder was horrible but, this theory sounded worse than hit-and-run murders or drive-bys. In Lottie's scenario, the killer actually took the time to bury the man. That felt...cold.

"If that were the case, wouldn't people have been looking for the victim?" Mom asked. "Hunters have their favorite spots, and I'd imagine family and close friends would know where those were. *Someone* had to have been searching for this poor man. And if that was one of his hunting spots, I can't imagine his remains would have gone undiscovered for so long."

"Do they even allow hunting in park lands?" I wondered. "I assumed the woods was part of the national park. But maybe the murder didn't happen in the woods. Maybe the murder happened in the field, and the killer took the body into the woods so it wouldn't be so easily found."

"Could be," Mom mused. "I wonder who owns that field the club was tracking in today?"

"Oh, that's Marcie Boarding's field," Lottie informed us.

I stared at her in surprise. "Marcie Boarding's field? The woman with the Doberman? She lost a tracking contest in *her own field*? That must really sting."

"Anything that's not a win for her and her dog stings Marcie Boarding," Lottie said with a wave of her hand. "But she doesn't actually farm that field or anything. Her husband owned a bunch of land and leased it out to farmers for hay or crops. He died six years ago, and Marcie never bothered to sell or lease any of the properties. They've all gone to weeds and thistle. Darned shame, if you ask me. Perfectly good hay fields going to waste like that."

Mom's eyes narrowed. "Maybe Marcie Boarding killed her husband six years ago and covered it up. Then she killed some other man who probably found out about her husband, and took care of him, burying him in the woods next to her property."

"That's quite a stretch, Mom," I pointed out.

"Plus, Jason died of prostate cancer," Lottie said. "I'm no oncologist, but I don't think someone can actually cause a man to have prostate cancer. Even if they could, it doesn't seem like an ideal way to kill someone."

"It's more likely that the woods were a convenient burial spot *because* of the unused field next to it," I said. "There aren't any houses near that area, and if the field isn't being farmed, then it would be unlikely that someone would stumble across the body. Someone in the Reckless Sniffers Club pointed out that the major trails are a good distance from that section of the woods, so it's equally unlikely another hiker would find the body. I did see a few hunting stands in a neighboring field, but they didn't look like they'd been in recent use."

"If there were hunting stands, then Lottie's idea of the hunting accident and cover-up seems like a possibility," Mom said. "A hunter goes to take his shot. Part of the rusted stand crumbles under him, and his shot goes wide, hitting another hunter. The man panics, and buries the victim."

I frowned. My knowledge of hunting and guns was pretty minimal, but I didn't think someone was supposed to shoot with another hunter that close to their prey. Although a hunter that careless might be the sort of person who'd bury their victim rather than report the accident to the police.

Mom sighed. "There's another possible explanation that doesn't involve foul play."

I nodded, somber at the reminder. "Self-inflicted gunshot wound."

Sometimes people went into the woods to die. And some of those people took guns with them. It still didn't explain what had looked like a shallow grave, but I wasn't at all an expert on these things. The dirt over the man's remains might have been due to some sort of natural occurrence. And his gun might be nearby, not revealed by Elvis's digging.

As shocking as it had been to see Elvis come out of the woods with that bone, this death might have not been murder. Until Stef, and the police, ruled it as a homicide, then all we were doing was indulging in gossip and conjecture.

Mom, Lottie, and I continued to chat, talk shifting from the dead body to Elvis's and my debut performance with the Reckless Sniffers Club. Both my friend and my mother encouraged me to take more time to get back to what had been a favorite hobby prior to my cancer diagnosis, and I promised to start training once more with Elvis. We'd gotten into a comfortable routine with the campground, and while there were still busy days, I now found myself with free time to hike, relax on the dock with a book, or even take a kayak out for a quick paddle.

After Lottie headed home, I ran back to the house and dug my scentwork box and six metal buckets out of the closet. Then I relieved Mom at the camp store and got to work. We currently didn't have any customers, and the basic training I'd planned could easily be done right in front of the store where I could pause if a guest wanted to buy supplies or order a food delivery for tomorrow.

Opening the small yellow tacklebox, I took out a vial of clove oil, a pair of disposable gloves, a cotton ball, a small glass jelly jar, and a perforated metal tin. Donning the disposable gloves, I tore the cotton ball in two and held the sections in one hand, carefully adding a drop of clove oil to each. Setting the vial aside, I used the tweezers to put one half of the cotton ball in the glass jar, and another in the perforated metal tin. Returning the tweezers and the vial to the tackle box, I took off the disposable gloves and walked around the side of the camp store to toss them in the dumpster.

Back on the porch, I put a dot on the tin with the scented cotton ball with a Sharpie marker, and used a set of tongs to place it into one of the metal buckets. In the other five buckets I placed empty metal tins, wanting Elvis to use his nose to find the scented tin, and not just assume a tin in a bucket meant he'd located the target.

That done, I walked down to the grassy area and set the six buckets in a line, making a mental note of which one contained the scented tin.

"Is this a game for tonight?" a young voice asked from behind me. "Or a craft project?"

I turned and saw Allie and Ellie Finn. They were ten-year-old twins, camping with their father, Carter Finn, in an impressively elaborate tent setup. Carter was a widower at forty, having tragically lost his wife five years ago when she was cycling and had been hit by a drunk driver. He'd told me they'd always been an outdoorsy family even before Cassidy's death, and he was determined to introduce the girls to all the activities he and his wife had loved.

The girls were absolutely on board with this, happily helping cook food over a firepit, decorating their bedroom tents and the dining tent with festive lights and cut out paper animals. They hiked, bird watched, swam, fished, and had an impressive collection of pressed flowers and leaves in their "plant identification" binders. I'd never met such enthusiastic, cheerful children, and I struggled to tell them apart with their identical brown ponytails and hazel eyes.

"It's a game I'm going to play with Elvis…" I squinted at the pair. "Allie."

She giggled. "I'm *Ellie*."

Noted. Ellie in the tan shorts with the blue tie-dye shirt, and Allie in the brown shorts with the dancing-tacos T-shirt.

"Elvis is a tracking dog, but we had to take some time off and now he needs a refresher course," I told the two girls. "So we're going to play a game, and every time he gets the right bucket, he gets a treat."

"Ooo, can we play?" Allie hopped up and down, clapping her hands. "I love Elvis."

"I love Elvis too," her sister chimed in.

Everyone loved Elvis. He was the star of the campground. Every week, our new guests made a huge fuss over how handsome he was, stroking his velvety ears, scratching his back, and plying him with snacks. The kids especially adored him, and would randomly appear at the store throughout the day asking if Elvis could come out to play fetch with the ball, or tug-of-war with a rope toy, or just sprawl on the grass to be cuddled and petted. My hound relished the adoration. He was always friendly, but was especially affectionate and tolerant when it came to children.

"You both can absolutely help," I told them. "If I was just starting to train Elvis, we'd tell him to 'find' and take him from bucket to bucket, letting him stick his nose in each of them. When we got to the right one, we'd reward him with a treat. That's how he'd begin to associate the scent with a reward. Elvis is trained, so what we're going to do is reward him with a treat when he indicates on the right bucket."

"The one with the dot on the tin is the right bucket?" Allie asked, peering down into the bucket.

"Yep. I'll let him sniff the cotton ball inside this jar, then tell him 'find.' He should go to each bucket and put his nose in, then sit when he finds the correct one. He only gets the treat for the correct bucket, so if he sits for the wrong one, we just wait. After a few seconds, he'll realize that he made a mistake, and keep sniffing."

"What if he keeps sitting at the wrong buckets?" Ellie asked.

"Then we backtrack and start rewarding him at the correct bucket, whether he indicates by sitting or not," I told them. Hopefully Elvis wouldn't need that remedial of training, though.

Allie clapped her hands together. "Let's do this! I'm so excited."

I left the girls outside and went in to get Elvis, clipping his leash on to lead him out. After a few minutes of affection and socializing with Ellie and Allie, we were ready to begin. Elvis sniffed the contents of the jar. I unclipped his leash, and asked him to "find."

The hound took off, sniffing the ground around the porch, making me realize that his search and rescue training was definitely stronger than his scent detection training.

Ellie giggled. "Over here, Elvis! Over here!"

She pointed to the buckets, and Elvis ran toward her, sticking his nose in the first bucket. From there he seemed to remember the routine, going from bucket to bucket before sitting down and looking at me expectantly.

"Yay!" Both girls cheered and clapped their hands.

"Free," I told Elvis. He ran over to me and I confirmed that he was a good boy, giving him a dog biscuit from my pocket.

We did this a few times with varying levels of success. After a dozen times, it was clear that Elvis was getting bored with the activity, so I put everything away and let the girls play fetch with him while I helped customers in the store. I was closing things down for the evening, hanging up the "call if you need something" sign when Carter came by to retrieve his daughters for dinner.

"I hope they weren't bothering you," he said with a smile as the girls threw the ball one last time for Elvis.

"Not at all. We did some scent detection training with Elvis and I think they really enjoyed it." I glanced at the two chasing my hound in circles, attempting to get the ball from him. "It's good exercise for him, and he loves playing with kids."

"They're missing their dog, Pumpkin," Carter told me. "They'll probably try to train him the same stuff when they get home. I'm not sure how well he'll do though. Pumpkin is a pug mix. He's happy to have them put tutus and hats on him, or paint his toenails, but I can't see him being good at scent detection."

"There's a French bulldog in the local tracking club," I mentioned. "He does pretty well with a size and breed handicap, so don't write Pumpkin off yet. He may surprise you. And either way, I'm sure he'll love the attention."

"True." He laughed. "Well, I need to get these two back to the campsite. We're grilling corn, and cooking the fish we caught today along with some veggies in foil packets."

"Yum." I glanced once more at the girls. "Are you all going fishing again tomorrow morning? I might do some search and rescue practice with Elvis and think the girls might get a kick out of that. It's basically hide-and-seek. They'd each need to put one of their dirty socks in a labeled Ziplock bag for Elvis to get a scent. Then they'd hide and I'd send Elvis out to find the one whose sock I had him smell."

"Poor Elvis." Carter shook his head. "I wouldn't want to have to smell those socks. Do you think he could tell them apart? They're identical twins. I don't know if that means they both smell the same or not."

"I really don't know. That might be an interesting thing to figure out, though."

He nodded. "We were going to do an early morning hike, but I could send them over around ten, if that works for you."

"That would be perfect," I told him. "And if something comes up, don't worry about it. We can always do our hide-and-seek activity another day."

"I think they'll enjoy this." He called to the girls and started down the porch steps. "They'll be here tomorrow morning, dirty socks in hand."

I called Elvis to me, and we both watched the girls and their father head back to the campsite. Elvis opened his mouth and the ball, wet with slobber, dropped to the porch with a thump. The hound looked at me expectantly, then glanced back and forth between me and the ball.

"Okay," I told him. "But only once. We've both got dinner waiting for us back at the house."

And then I planned on a relaxing evening. We'd both had a busy day, and I could think of nothing more appealing right now that watching television while sprawled on the couch with my dog.

CHAPTER 4

I was up with the sun the next day, gathering Elvis's tracking harness and leash as well as some special treats for the girls to reward him with once he'd found them. We took our usual pre-dawn walk around the campground, then got the coffee started and sorted the food Flora delivered at six.

Around nine, Mom stopped by to announce that she was heading out for her knitting club. Sunday was her day off, so instead of relieving me at ten like she usually did, she'd be spending the day making soft, colorful hats for newborns, cancer patients, and the homeless.

"Have fun," I said digging the SUV keys out of my pocket and extending them to her.

She held up her hand. "I've got a friend giving me a ride today. And I could be a little late coming back, if that's okay. We might grab a late lunch or dinner after."

"You know I never mind you taking the SUV," I told her. "Austin will have his truck here in case of an emergency, so it's not like I'll be stuck here without transportation."

Mom had steadfastly refused to purchase another vehicle

once her trusty Jetta had died three years ago, but back then we'd lived in town where most stores were a short walk away and both taxis and Ubers were plentiful. Here we were remote, and even if Mom wanted to walk the three miles in to town, she'd be taking her life in her hands on these winding country roads with no real shoulders. I never wanted her to feel awkward about driving the SUV, but I was thrilled she had found a friend.

"I know. Next week maybe I'll be the one giving my friend a ride," she said, heading outside with a wave.

I'm nosy, so I followed, tying Elvis to the porch railing. Then I looked around for something to do, finally making half-hearted efforts to pull weeds from between the walkway pavers. Mom had mentioned a few of the people who were in the knitting club, and others from her bridge club, but outside of those scheduled meetings, she hadn't met up with any of them. There hadn't been any lunches together, or coffee meet-ups, or even a trip to a local craft fair. In the last few months I'd found friends—really good friends—and while I hoped that Mom felt welcome joining Lottie, or Sierra, or Danielle and me, I really wanted her to find friends of her own. So I was excited that someone would be picking her up for today's knitting club.

And I couldn't wait to catch a glimpse of Mom's friend, and maybe get an introduction. She had seemed a little cagy about the whole thing, not telling me the friend's name or even indicating their gender. Was her new friend a man? I wasn't sure how I felt about that idea, to be honest. After Dad had died, Mom hadn't seemed interested in dating, but he'd passed a long time ago. Mom might be eighty-five, but she was healthy and fit. If she wanted to date, I wouldn't stand in her way.

But I most definitely would lurk around to catch a

glimpse of the guy as he was picking her up for the knitting club.

A giant diesel Mercedes sedan made its way carefully down the drive. The vehicle was old, but clearly had been well maintained. The chrome was polished, the black paint glossy and waxed within an inch of its life. I recognized the car even though I'd only seen it one other time—in a parking lot with a grouping of motorcycles and an old rusted truck.

I was pretty sure this Mercedes belonged to Rosalind, the woman that Mom and I had met at the Twelve Gauge last month.

The Twelve Gauge was a local dive bar, where illegal gambling, drunken fights, and even stabbings weren't rare occurrences. I was a bit afraid of the place, but Mom was fascinated. Last month we'd gone there on a Saturday at lunchtime, since she was dying to check it out and I wanted to ask the owner some questions—research for the motive behind a local murder. Lunch on a Saturday seemed to have less of a risk of violence then the Thursday night trivia contest Mom had really wanted to attend, so we'd gone. Mom had befriended the three bikers as well as a woman about her age who'd been drinking Jim Beam and soda at the end of the bar.

Rosalind. I hadn't assumed she was the sort of woman who'd be interested in knitting projects for charity, but clearly I needed to check my assumptions and prejudices at the dive-bar door.

I'd been back to the Twelve Gauge only once since then. Lottie, who'd felt left out at Mom's and my visit, had talked me into going with her on a Tuesday night. The crowd had been rowdy and loud, but thankfully no stabbings or bar fights had occurred. I'd actually enjoyed myself, but had been procrastinating on going with Mom to Thursday night trivia, citing our campground's turnover night as an excuse.

Watching the Mercedes pull into the parking area, I wondered if Mom had been going there with her new friend on her time off. It wasn't any of my business what my mother did, but I felt a little sad at the thought that my delays and excuses might have meant she'd turn to Rosalind for her trivia team, tired of waiting for me to agree to go.

"I'm off, Sassy," Mom called out with a wave. "I'll text you if I'm going to be late."

"Have a great time." I walked a few steps over and waved at the woman in the driver's seat of the Mercedes with her silver hair in a severe bun, thick blue eyeshadow on her lids and false eyelashes so long they practically touched her eyebrows. "Hi Rosalind. Nice to see you again."

The woman glance at me, nodded, then turned to say something to my mom, who was climbing into the passenger side of the car. I wasn't insulted at the curt greeting. I got the feeling that Rosalind was a bit of a loner, and the fact that my mom had managed to befriend her was probably something of a miracle.

Or not. Mom had a way of making friends even with the most unlikely of people. She was so cheerful, such a good listener, and absolutely unjudgmental and accepting of anyone's personality and lifestyle. I loved her for that, and I knew that others did as well.

Waving as the Mercedes turned around and headed back down the drive, I saw two little girls headed my way, each holding a plastic Ziploc bag.

"We're ready for hide-and-seek with Elvis," the girl with the pink baseball cap announced.

"And Elvis is ready for you…" I squinted, "Allie."

She giggled. "I'm Ellie."

Right. Ellie with the pink ball cap. Allie with the purple shirt.

Behind me Elvis let out a whine that ended in a high-pitched howl. The girls took off for him, dropping their Ziploc bags and greeting the hound with hugs and pets. I gathered up the bags, noting that they'd done as I requested. Each bag had a name printed on the front in Sharpie, and held a sock—a very dirty sock.

Putting the bags on the porch, I went inside and got Elvis's tracking harness and forty-foot leash. Once Elvis was outfitted, I told the girls to go hide, letting them know that I'd give them five minutes before I sent Elvis after one of them.

To keep the hound from seeing them hide, I took him inside the camp store. We stood behind the register, where only I could see the girls through the window as they raced around for the best hiding places. There I kept Elvis occupied with a tug toy until I no longer saw the girls and five minutes had passed.

We went back to the porch and I clipped his long leash on.

"Work," I told him. The hound sat, attentive with his ears forward.

Picking up the Ziploc bag that said Ellie, I opened it and extended it toward Elvis. "Work."

He shoved his nose in the bag and snuffled loudly. I knew he could probably smell the sock outside of the bag. Heck, he could probably smell that sock from clear inside the camp store, but the hound seemed to enjoy really immersing himself in the olfactory experience.

When I felt he'd had more than enough time to gather the scent, I pulled the bag away and commanded him to "find." The hound rose, immediately dropping his head to the porch and sniffing in a back-and-forth pattern. He continued this down the steps and around the area in front of the camp store, coming to an abrupt halt as he caught the scent. His tail began to wag. Then his whole body began to wag. With a low excited whine, Elvis took off, his nose glued to the ground.

We took a circuitous path around the parking area that I recognized from watching the girls race around earlier. Every now and then Elvis would hesitate, circling around and working back and forth until he found the scent trail once more. We looped around two cabins, across the drive, and along the edge of the woods. Near the bathhouse, Elvis began to bay, scenting the air this time as he ran for the building.

We rounded the corner, and a girl squealed in delight. Elvis's entire body vibrated and he sniffed her, wiggling as she rubbed his ears. But there was only one problem—the girl Elvis had found wasn't Ellie. This was Allie with her purple shirt and braids.

"He was supposed to find your sister," I told her. "I guess that answers the question of whether identical twins smell the same to a dog or not."

Allie laughed. "Elvis found the right person. Ellie and I thought we'd trick you by putting the wrong names on the bags. The one that says Ellie is actually my sock, and Ellie's sock is in the bag labeled Allie. Ellie is hiding at the edge of the woods behind that rock. Elvis went right by her and came to find me instead. So he *can* tell us apart!"

"Smart dog," I praised the hound, scratching his back. "And smart girls. Shall we get Ellie and play again?"

We continued the hide-and-seek game with only the occasional interruption to ring up a guest's purchases. At noon, the girls' father came to collect them for lunch and Elvis happily plopped down on his cushion behind the counter to nap. He was clearly tired, but he hadn't once found the wrong girl in our games today. If anything, the hide-and-seek game confirmed what I'd already known—Elvis preferred searching for people far more than he did identifying which tin held the pine or clove scented cotton ball. I didn't blame him. Finding lost people did seem a lot more interesting than a cotton ball, and the reward of a happy child was greater than any treat I could give him for a successful scent detection round.

Elvis snoozed and I restocked shelves, checked inventory, and went over activities for the week. Sunday wasn't a busy day for the campground aside from the typical morning rush at the camp store and it didn't make sense for me to stand around inside the store all day when my guests were out and about. Elvis had gotten his exercise for the day and so had I. There wasn't anything else for me to do in the camp store, but there were plenty of other things to do around the campground.

Austin had come in at ten o'clock to check the camp and RV sites for any hookup issues or trash-dumping needs, then had trimmed and mowed before the sun had gotten too intense. When he'd finished that, he'd gone over to the boathouse to clean and prep the two boats. It was past time they earned their keep, and I hoped that once they were clean and launched, I could use them to earn some extra money for the campground.

I'd taken a quick look at the cobweb-covered, dusty boats when I'd first bought the campground, but it had been early April and I'd had my hands full with other matters. The canoes and kayaks were fully rented every day during the summer season, but I knew there were plenty of people who would be willing to pay for a fast-and-fun inner-tube ride behind the speed boat. Or people who would pay for a leisurely cruise while a local historian talked about the formation of Savage Lake and the various communities and folklore of the area. Sunset cruises with wine and charcu-terie. Ghost tours on the water. A guided tour showing the best fishing spots. Or just a lazy day on the water with someone else driving the boat.

I'd paid for these boats as part of my purchase of the campground. Might as well start to make some money off of them.

I grabbed a bottle of water out of the fridge, checked to make sure Elvis was fast asleep on his cushion, then headed toward the boathouse. Austin had the huge, sliding barn doors open. The pontoon boat had been pulled out of the boat house and was on a giant trailer with some rapidly deflating tires. I eyed the tires, wondering if they could be patched, and how much it might cost to replace them. Although once the boat was in the water, we wouldn't need to worry about trailer tires until fall since I had a dock with slips for four boats.

The pressure washer was hooked up beside the boat, and from the puddles of water around it, it was clear that Austin had been hard at work. The pontoon boat looked clean and tidy. It seemed in good repair, although the stripes on the canopy had faded from what had once been indigo and red to baby blue and pink.

"It looks great," I called out to Austin who was in the boathouse looking at the other vessel. "Do you think we can launch it this week?"

"We can launch it, but unless you're wanting to do the Viking-row-thing, it's not going anywhere." Austin walked out of the boathouse, wiping his hands on the bottom of his T-shirt. "The motor's gone."

I blew out a breath. "Is it something that can be fixed or do we need to buy a new one? It probably sat in the boathouse for almost a year, so maybe the motor just needs a tune-up or something?"

"No, it's *gone*," Austin corrected me. "There's no motor. The pontoon boat had an outboard and it's not there."

I stared at the boat, dismayed. There went my hopes of historic lake tours and sunset cruises. How much did outboard motors cost? This pontoon was much larger than the fishing boat Jake towed down my boat launch every few days, so I was assuming it would need a much larger motor than the one he had. Hundreds of dollars? Thousands of dollars? I knew next to nothing about boats and had no idea.

"How about the speed boat?" I asked, glancing at the Baycraft still in the boathouse.

"I haven't checked that one over yet. Let me get it out and take a look." Austin went to his truck and hooked the trailer up, removing the chucks that blocked the trailer wheels before pulling the boat out of the shelter.

I stared at the old speed boat. It looked worse than the pontoon boat, but it hadn't been pressure washed yet. Maybe once it was cleaned up...

It was June and campers were wanting to enjoy not just the hiking trails and the quaint town of Reckless, but all that Savage Lake had to offer. And while Savage Lake was holding up its end of that bargain, Reckless Camper Campground wasn't. I needed these boats to work. I'd preferred it be the pontoon boat, but if this one ran, then it was better than nothing.

While I could get twelve people on the pontoon boat, I could only have four to six on the Baycraft. It would make any historic lake tours less profitable, but I could at least use it for inner tube rides.

"It's really not that bad, Miss Sassy," Austin said, clearly seeing my expression.

It *was* that bad. I walked around the boat only to halt, nearly coming to tears as I saw a hole in the fiberglass, right where the waterline would come.

A fiberglass repair might be cheaper than replacing an outboard motor, though. I glanced over at Austin.

"Does it start?" I asked.

"I haven't tried yet."

Austin looked under what I was calling the "hood" and connected the battery. Then he checked the clearance of the propeller, climbed on the boat, and inserted the key. With a quick twist of the ignition, I heard the motor catch, start, then sputter out.

"Think it just needs a little work, Miss Sassy," Austin called out.

"Even if we get the engine running, there's still a hole in the side of the boat." Was that starboard or port? I couldn't remember.

Austin came around the side towards me. "Yeah, that's gonna be a big problem. You might want to have it hauled to the marina for that kind of thing. I'm no expert, but I've been boating on this lake my whole life and in my opinion, you don't want to cheap out on a fiberglass repair."

Figures. If I was going to haul this thing into the marina, then I might as well have them tune up the motor too. It would be horrible if the boat died on me out in the middle of Savage Lake with guests on board.

"What about the pontoon boat?" Austin asked. "It's in good shape. I think we'd be ready to go if you got a motor for it."

I thought about that a second. "Are you licensed to drive...or sail...or pilot. Whatever the term is for legally being able to drive a boat?"

I wanted to take classes and get my license, since it would probably be important for insurance reasons for me to be certified to drive guests on these boats. But if Austin was already licensed, then maybe he could drive until I got a license of my own.

Austin bit back a smile. "I got my captain's license at sixteen. I've been boating since I was eight with my parents supervising. I'm big on safety, so you can absolutely trust me to take your campers out onto the lake. But we can't do that with a boat that doesn't have a motor."

I sighed. "I need to run the numbers and see what I can afford. I'd rather get the pontoon boat up and running, though."

I was disappointed that neither of the boats was water ready, but I was a glass-half-full sort of person. Actually, I was a pour-it-in-a-smaller-glass-and-call-it-full person. A few potholes in the road of life weren't going to keep Sassy Letouroux from reaching her destination, so instead of fretting, I thought about all the good things that had happened in the last year.

I owned the campground where I'd experienced some of my favorite childhood memories. Spring had come early and the weather so far this year had been fantastic. The one heavy storm we'd had hadn't damaged the campground in any significant way, and the campers had come through it with good humor. We were fully booked and the previous guests this year had been complimentary about the new management and little extras Mom and I had implemented. According to Mom's numbers, we were on track to increase revenue over last year, and that would be key to turning this old campground around. The canoes and kayaks were in demand. Amenities, including bait for fishing, were flying off the camp store shelves and food orders were strong and steady. Friday night bonfires were a huge hit as were the quirky themed parties and activities I'd come up with to entertain both our younger and our older guests.

I'd beaten cancer.

"We'll get one of these boats in the water and running before the end of the season," Austin vowed.

I turned to the teen, adding him to my list of blessings. Austin, was the hardest working young man I'd ever met outside of my father. He mowed and trimmed. He chopped wood. He repaired the docks, the outbuildings, and the cabin porches. The guests loved him. Mom loved him. Elvis, my bloodhound, loved him.

I'll admit that I loved him, too—like an adopted grandson. I'd already increased his pay last month. And if he kept working like he was, that boy was going to absolutely get another raise.

"I'm not happy about that missing motor on the pontoon boat," Austin continued, his expression grim. "I searched the boathouse and the garage for it, thinking that maybe Mr. Trout pulled it off to fix it, but it's just gone. Do you think he sent it out for repair?"

"I don't really know. It wasn't noted as out for repair in the documents I got when I was buying the campground," I told him.

In the campground inventory, the outboard motor had been listed as being attached to the pontoon boat. That meant it had been there as of January when the estate auditors had gone over the business assets and Len Trout's sons had listed the campground for sale. If Len had pulled the motor and taken it for repairs, it wouldn't have been on that list. I'd still check the records to see if the motor was sitting at the marina or a local repair shop, waiting for someone to pick it up, but I doubted that was the case. Everyone in Reckless and in neighboring Savage knew I'd bought the campground. If they had a motor that they'd repaired, that needed picking up and paying for, they probably would have reached out before now.

I was afraid the motor was gone—as in stolen, gone.

The boathouse had been locked. Of all the people who'd had keys, only one of them had motive for stealing a used outboard motor. My former handyman.

I'd never met Daryl Butts—well, except for finding him

dead on the floor of one of my cabins within hours of closing on the campground and taking possession of the property. When I'd called 911, I'd no idea who he was. Actually, I'd had no idea he was even there until Mom told me there was a dead body in one of the cabins.

The guy had accrued some rather alarming gambling debts, and had been trying to steal an antique book in a scam to sell it and pay off his debts. It wasn't a stretch to think he'd been the one to steal the outboard, especially since he was the only one besides Len Trout's heirs who had keys to all the buildings.

And to think I'd almost planted a memorial tree and placed a plaque on the campground honoring the man. No memorial tree for you, Daryl Butts, you thieving jerk.

"If you see a used motor for sale somewhere at a reasonable price, let me know," I told Austin.

No motor meant no boat. And as salty as I was about its possible theft, there was really no recourse at this point. I'd just need to suck it up and figure out how to scrape together money for a new one.

In the meantime, I'd continue encourage canoe and kayak rentals. Our busy season was only until the end of August with a rapidly declining tail of business through October. We definitely needed to make money while the sun shined, because winter would either see the seasonal closure of the campground, or a severely reduced amount of guests. The money we made now needed to help us last through the off season, and give us enough funds to start up again next spring.

There were so many opportunities for expansion with this campground. Winter cabin rentals were one. Increasing activities on the lake were another.

Savage Lake was enormous with two bridges at either end, providing access to towns on the other side without the need to drive for over an hour around the lake. Even with the bridges it took thirty minutes to reach Derwood or Red Rock by car where it would be a ten-minute boat ride. Although my main ideas were lake-history tours, sunset cruises, and lake-ghost tours, I'd also thought about a ferry service for my guests. There were some fun brew pubs on the other side of the lake, and Derwood had a public marina with a cute downtown area an easy walking distance away. A ferry service might provide extra revenue and possibly a popular service for my guests.

"I'll keep my eyes open for a motor, Miss Sassy," Austin vowed. "Do you want me to get quotes for the speed boat repairs?"

I thought about that for a second. "Right now I'm going to focus on the pontoon boat. Let's get that up and running first. The speed boat can probably wait until next year, but I really want to get the pontoon boat in the water as soon as possible."

I had plans for the pontoon boat. And while I also had plans for the Baycraft, those plans didn't seem as lucrative as the pontoon boat ones If I had to choose between the two boats, it would be the pontoon one.

Austin nodded. "I might ask a couple of my friends to come over and take a look at the Baycraft, just to get an idea of what it might need. It's a sweet boat, and I hate to see it just sitting in this garage gathering dust."

"Go ahead, but just know that I probably don't have the budget to get the Baycraft up and running this year," I warned him.

He saluted. "Got it."

Austin turned back around and continued power-washing the boats while I headed back to the campground office.

CHAPTER 5

J worked in the camp store until three o'clock, updating records and sending the food orders for tomorrow morning. Once that was done, I dug through both the computerized records and the tons of documents I'd gotten when I bought the campground, searching for some sign of where my missing boat motor might be. Sadly, everything I read indicated the motor should still be attached to the boat.

As much as I wanted to point the finger at my former handyman, I was well aware that a lot of the campground's flaws had been glossed over at closing. There was a chance that the estate auditor had glanced in the garage, seen two boats, and just assumed the motor was there.

In the end, it really didn't matter. I could be mad at Daryl Butts, or some auditor, or even Len Trout's sons, but none of that was going to bring the motor back. Rather than waste time and energy being mad, I needed to do something productive. So I put the paperwork aside and watched a few YouTube videos on drywall repair for an hour before heading outside to sit on the porch with Elvis.

I was two chapters into my book when I heard the sound of an outboard motor coming up the lake toward the campground. Elvis jumped up from his pillow, tail wagging furiously as he looked out at the boat. I recognized it, but even if I hadn't, Elvis's excitement clearly told me who the boat belonged to.

It was Jake, coming back from a day of fishing.

I smiled as I watched the boat slow, easing its way past my docks toward the boat launch. Jake had approached me a few months ago and asked if he could pay for access to the lake via my boat launch. He wanted to do more fishing this year, and his property wasn't lakefront. The public launch was a good distance away, where mine was conveniently down the lane and across the road from his property. I'd refused payment, telling the sometimes-deputy that he was welcome to use the launch any time he wanted. Jake had taken me up on that offer, and was here pretty much every other day, heading out close to dawn and coming back in the afternoon. I couldn't see that he caught a lot of fish, but I think it was the relaxation on the water that was the real appeal. Fish were a bonus.

I flipped the sign on the store to closed, and unhooked Elvis, watching him race his way across the lawn toward the boat launch. I made a more leisurely way over, amused to see Elvis standing at the water's edge, baying as Jake brought his boat in.

I waved. He waved. Then I stood next to Elvis and kept the hound from bothering Jake as he pulled his boat onto the ramp. The man jumped out, tied the boat off, then greeted Elvis and me before heading off to get his truck and trailer. I grabbed Elvis's collar and hauled him over to the side so Jake could back the trailer down the ramp and into the water. He set the truck in park and hopped out, getting back in the boat and starting the engine.

I told Elvis to stay and untied the rope, tossing it to Jake. He eased the boat onto the trailer and I hooked the front line to the winch. Jake cut the motor and lifted it, then got out and took over, winching the boat further up the trailer before beginning to secure it in place.

"You know, it would be a lot easier if you just docked your boat in one of my slips," I told him as I assisted.

"I don't want to take up one of your slips," he protested. "You've got two boats of your own, and there might be guests of yours who are renting from the marina."

Two boats of my own. Yeah…about that…

"No guests have rented anything besides my canoes and kayaks," I told him. "I've got four slips, none of which I'm using at the moment, and you're here every other day as it is. It would save you having to hook the trailer up and launch the boat every time you want to go fishing. You can just drive down the mountain, get in, and take off."

He hesitated, looking at me a few seconds before he returned to securing his boat. "I'll think about it. Certainly would save me some time, and I might actually go out every day if my boat was at a slip, but I don't want to inconvenience you. If you're still interested and I decide I want to do it, then I need to pay you a fair price. You tend to undercharge, Sassy, and I don't want to take advantage of you just because we're friends."

"I'm not making a dime off those slips right now," I argued. "And I'm not likely to anytime in the future. I might as well allow a friend to use them. What are friends for if not to help each other out?"

He laughed. "Okay. Let me think about it."

We worked in silence for a few moments until the boat was secure. Jake pulled the trailer from the water, then to my surprise he stopped, shutting off the truck and getting out.

"I see you're getting your own boats out and ready," Jake

said as he walked around toward me. "Austin did a nice job of cleaning the pontoon boat up."

"Well, they're nothing but lawn ornaments right now," I grumbled. "The pontoon boat needs a motor, and the speedboat needs fiberglass repairs. We can't get it started, either."

Jake's expression was full of sympathy. "Boats are money pits. Seems there's always something you're needing to fix."

I blew out an exasperated breath. "I was hoping to at least be able to use the pontoon boat for lake cruises."

I'd had plans for the speed boat as well, but those might have to wait. Besides the repairs, I wasn't sure about insurance liability when it came to taking people on high-speed inner tube or wave board rides. Plus, there would probably be a steeper learning curve in learning to drive the speed boat. Even though I'd need a license to drive the pontoon boat as well, it didn't intimidate me like the Baycraft did.

Jake looked over toward where the boats were parked in front of the garage. "How bad is the motor on the pontoon boat? It might be quicker and cheaper to repair it."

"Oh, there's no repairing it," I informed him. "It's gone. Vanished. Not there. Can't repair a missing motor."

His eyes widened. "It's gone?"

I scowled. "Someone must have stolen it. Or maybe Len sold it or junked it and never got around to buying a new one."

I hated that I leapt right to "stolen." Were all the murders lately turning me into one of those bitter people who saw everyone as a potential criminal? Would I soon be unable to see anything but the worst in humanity?

"Either way, I don't have a motor for the pontoon boat, and the speed boat is in need of some repair as well," I added.

"I'll keep my eyes open for a used outboard," Jake promised.

"Thanks." I was feeling bad about my sour mood. It had

been quite a week. Actually it had been quite a weekend. A less-than-ideal performance at the tracking event. A dead man in the woods. And now I'd discovered I was the owner of two worthless boats.

Speaking of the dead man in the woods...

"Were you all able to identify the remains Elvis found yesterday?" I asked him.

Jake shook his head. "Not yet. There was no ID, and what was left of the clothes didn't help. Stef was able to provide an estimate on his height along with an approximate window for his death, but we'll need to wait on identification until we run the DNA." Jake rolled his eyes. "There are a ton of rumors going around right now that the remains are of a man who went missing a year ago, but we have no proof of that."

"Someone local went missing a year ago?" It sounded reasonable to assume that a body in the woods might be that missing person, but Jake didn't seem convinced. "What are the rumors? Who was this missing person?" I prodded.

Jake hesitated.

I wanted more information, but I didn't want to seem like a Nosy Nancy. Oh, what the heck. He already knew I was a Nosy Nancy. Might as well not try to pretend differently.

"Come on, Jake. Who is this missing person?" I finally asked.

He sighed. "There's probably no harm in telling you since Lottie will most likely be over here in an hour or two with more information than anyone in the Sheriff's department has. A man went missing around June or July last year, which is when Stef is estimating the time of death for the remains Elvis found in the woods. Because the dates overlap, everyone in town is now convinced the dead man in the woods is Buddy Hooper."

The name meant nothing to me since I'd just moved here less than three months ago.

"You never found any trace of this Buddy Hooper?" I asked. "Were there any calls from his cell phone after he went missing? Any withdrawals from his bank account? Anything charged to his credit card that might give you an idea of where he went?"

Jake grimaced. "This isn't Law and Order, Sassy. He didn't have any family freaking out and filing missing persons reports, saying it wasn't like him to disappear. Buddy lived alone. He didn't have any close friends, and his romantic relationships were casual at best. He's a grown adult, and grown adults have the right to take off and move somewhere without having to notify everyone in town."

"But you said he was missing. So *someone* felt Buddy should have notified them if he was leaving," I countered. "You're not telling me you did nothing to search for this guy?"

Jake held up his hands. "We're a sheriff's department of two and a half covering the entire county. There's limited manpower to do a deep search for someone who might have just wanted to skip town and start fresh somewhere else. We asked around to see if anyone had heard from him or knew where he went to. We checked to see if his truck had been involved in any accidents or was found abandoned somewhere, then we let it go."

I stared at him. "Let it go? A man goes missing and just because he doesn't have any family banging on your door to look for him, you just let it go?"

"Two thirds of missing adults are missing voluntarily," he countered. "If you discount the silver alerts where at-risk seniors wander off, that percentage goes up. Sometimes people are fleeing a bad marriage. Sometimes people hate their job and are having financial trouble, and just want a fresh start somewhere else. Buddy wasn't good with his money. He'd been on the edge of eviction a bunch of times and was being evicted when he disappeared. It's not a stretch to think he'd want to duck out on his debts."

"Oh." Again I'd jumped to conclusions, seeing foul play everywhere. Jake was a professional, and if he thought this guy just skipped town to avoid paying debts, then he was probably right. "Did he have any family at all you might have contacted? I'm assuming even a person like this Buddy would have family who'd worried when he didn't show up for Sunday dinner or something."

"He's got a brother in Florida, but they hadn't spoken to each other in years," Jake told me. "He lived alone, didn't have any close friends, didn't have a regular girlfriend that we're aware of. No one raised the alarm for roughly a month. A couple of people complained that he hadn't shown up with a hay delivery, which had happened before. It wasn't enough to set off any alarms. His landlord had been in the process of evicting him for unpaid rent, so it also didn't set off any alarms when the landlord and Sean had to put Buddy's belongings roadside. It wasn't until no one had seen him for a month that people began to wonder. He'd lived in Reckless for about a decade. Everyone just assumed he up and moved and didn't let anyone know. Eventually one of his romantic partners came in and said that she was concerned. Even she admitted that he had made comments about leaving town for some business. That plus the missing hay deliveries and the eviction gave us enough cause to nose around and ask questions. But there was no sign of foul play. We didn't find anything that led us to believe something bad had happened to him."

"Wait, he was renting?" I asked as Jake's comments about eviction sunk in. "From a landlord?" I frowned, confused. "I thought he was a farmer with the hay deliveries and all. How was he selling hay if he was renting an apartment in downtown Reckless?"

Jake chuckled. "Not everyone who rents is in an apartment. There's quite a few people who lease out their acreage for another farmer to plant or use as pasture. And there are farms that for one reason or another are up for lease. Land is expensive and farming is a business with a lot of risks. If someone loses their farm and that's the only job they've ever known, then their options are working as a farmhand for someone else, or renting a farm and hoping to eventually make enough to purchase again."

"Renting a farm? That can't be cheap," I said.

"Cheaper than owning one sometimes." Jake reached down to scratch Elvis's head. "Buddy wasn't a complete loser. I had a couple of bad experiences with him, but he was a hard worker and he made decent money with his hay and side businesses. If you kept an eye on him and held him accountable, it was worth it to buy from him."

Side businesses. I immediately wondered if one of those side businesses was what got him killed—because like the gossip mill in town, I felt that the similarities in the timelines between Buddy's disappearance and the dead man's demise were too much of a coincidence to rule out they were one and the same person.

"If Buddy was a hard worker bringing in good money, then why was he being evicted from the farm he was leasing?" I wondered.

Jake shrugged. "He drove a nice expensive truck. He had a loan for his tractor. There was equipment he had to buy, and some people just seem to have a problem budgeting. Besides that, I know Buddy had a habit of not paying things until the last minute. He'd let a few months go without paying his rent, then bring everything up to date when the landlord filed for eviction. Most people just figured it was his way of screwing over the landlord, but others said Buddy wasn't frugal with money and that he often had a cash flow problem."

"I can't imagine why the landlord would continue to rent to him after the lease was up," I said.

"Who knows? Maybe it was hard to find tenants for a farm that size? Or he figured since Buddy always eventually paid that it was a better scenario than having the farm empty for months and incur the expense of finding a new tenant?"

"So you're talking to the landlord?" I asked. "And the people who Buddy'd ripped off in the months prior to his disappearance? Just in case this dead man is him?"

Jake looked toward the heavens. "No, Sassy. First, I'm an on-call deputy, so any investigation on my part has to be authorized by the Sheriff. Secondly, it would be premature to dig into Buddy Hooper's affairs when we don't even know if the remains are his. For all we know, the dead man was an out-of-state hiker, someone who was killed in a hunting accident, or he was a victim of a random murder. Or it could have been someone who was murdered elsewhere in the state and just transported here to a dump site."

"But Buddy Hooper vanished the same time this man was probably killed," I argued. "Doesn't that alone necessitate looking further into his disappearance?"

"As I said, we nosed around when people realized Buddy hadn't been seen in a while and we found no sign of foul play." Jake sighed. "It's not a crime to leave a town and not let anyone know where you're going, Sassy. Grown people have the right to privacy and the right to move around without the police tracking them down all the time."

I guessed he was right. Still, if the body had been Buddy Hooper, then the sooner someone started digging into the man's past, the better. It had already been a year since his disappearance, and the longer it went, the less likely it was that there would be any clues left to follow. Plus, if the rumors were racing through the town that Buddy's body had been found, the killer would have ample time to make sure his tracks were covered. The killer would know that the body was Buddy's and he, or she, would make sure there was nothing left to trace the murder back to them.

"Buddy wasn't the most dependable guy in Reckless," Jake added. "He wasn't a horrible person, but he *was* sneaky and dishonest when it came to business dealings. If he could skim a little of the top or scam someone, he'd do it. It wasn't really a surprise that he ran out on a bunch of debts without leaving a forwarding address."

It totally made sense, and I felt like an idiot for jumping on the gossip train and making assumptions.

"Reckless is a small town. I'm guessing everyone learned not to do business with Buddy if he had a habit of scamming people and not paying his debts," I commented.

"Not really." Jake laughed. "Everyone learned to double check what he was delivering, and to not pay until every last item had been accounted and looked over, and to get large deposits up front if he was buying something. If Buddy promised fifty bales of hay, you might get forty-eight, or the bales might be ten percent smaller than they should be. He wasn't breaking into people's houses and robbing them, or getting paid and not delivering at all. It was more little stuff—stuff that wasn't bad enough to get him arrested or even for most people to bother taking him to court on it. I think he just got in over his head with debt, that it all started adding up over the years into an amount that he couldn't pay."

"But why would anyone bother dealing with him at all if you couldn't trust him?" I asked. "Surely there were other people who could deliver hay?"

Jake shrugged. "There are other farmers in the area with

hay to sell, but there's a finite quantity. Buddy had hay to sell at a good price, you just had to watch him like a hawk."

"Sounds like the voice of someone who had personal experience with the guy," I teased, thinking that Jake with his horses had a clear need to buy hay.

"Totally. And Buddy wasn't above trying to short a delivery to a former cop who is an on-call local deputy either," Jake told me.

I nodded in sympathy. "So if that body isn't Buddy's, then whose is it? Any guesses?"

"No guesses." Jake shrugged. "Hopefully there will be a match on the DNA. If not, then there will be a whole lot of old-fashioned police work, checking missing persons reports from that time period. We'll have to wait and see where the evidence leads us."

"But it's definitely murder? Or does Stef think this might be a suicide?" I was clearly fishing, but Jake's smile told me he didn't mind my curiosity.

"Stef hasn't completely ruled suicide out. Judging from the bullet wound, it's not likely to have been a hunting accident, but she's not completely ruling that out either," Jake said.

I thought about that for a second. "I'm guessing that means the man wasn't killed by a rifle? So you're saying someone killed him with a pistol?"

"I'm not saying that at all," Jake protested. "Stef believes the man was shot at close range, and in my experience, most hunting accidents happen from a distance, or are things like your drunk friend shooting you in the foot while in a deer blind."

"Yikes," I exclaimed, wondering how many drunken hunter shoots friend in the foot cases Jake had to investigate in a given year. "What if a drunk hunter did somehow shoot his friend in the head? He'd probably panic, bury the man in a shallow grave and not report the accident?"

He shrugged. "It's a possibility, but even if that was what happened, the hunter still would have to stand trial for some degree of manslaughter as well as other charges like unregulated burial. A hunting accident that results in a death is at least manslaughter, covering it up makes it far more serious."

I thought back on those unsolved mysteries shows Mom and I loved to watch. "Do you really think you'll eventually find out what happened to him? Or even who he is?"

Jake sighed. "Honestly? I don't know. If there's no DNA match, we might never know who he was or find out what happened. But we'll keep looking even if we don't. There's always new technologies and new information that come along, and sometimes that helps us solve cold cases. So even if we hit a dead end now, in five years we could get a clue that helps us close the case. We cops never give up hope."

I nodded, thinking that I would do the same. I wouldn't give up hope. Since Elvis had been the one to find this body, I felt like I needed to do everything I could to help identify the dead man and figure out what happened to him.

It might take years, but I wouldn't give up either.

CHAPTER 6

J kept the "be back later" sign on the camp store and went with Elvis to the house. I wasn't sure if Mom would return home for dinner, so I left that up in the air, making up a batch of tuna salad for an early dinner. If Mom and Rosalind didn't go out to eat, she could have some of the tuna or warm up the leftover enchiladas from Friday.

At five o'clock, I decided I should return to the store. People would start returning from their hikes, fishing, or paddling soon and I wanted to be open if anyone needed to buy firewood, charcoal, or pick up a six pack of beer.

I was just turning the sign to "open" when I saw a familiar BMW sedan making its way down the drive. Lottie parked, hopped out, and speed-walked her way over to me. She was wearing a white A-line style tank dress with huge poppies printed all over it. I wasn't used to seeing her in a dress, or seeing the giant, red Lucite hoops in her ears.

"Coming from church?" I teased, wondering what had Lottie dressed to the nines on a Sunday evening.

"Actually, yes. I attended the early-bird service at Calvary Baptist in Derwood, the ten o'clock service at Shiloh Baptist in Savage, then caught the last half of the eleven o'clock at Reckless Reformed Baptist. I haven't been home to change clothes yet since after the last service, I had to check out three different community halls and a bed-and-breakfast in Derwood."

I stared. "Seriously? *Three* church services? That's a year's worth of religion in one day. Did you have a whole lot of repenting to do? Is this some kind of church bingo where you gain eternal salvation if you can fill your card in one week?"

Lottie snorted. "It's wedding stuff. We're members of Reckless Reformed, but Amanda asked me to check out the other Baptist churches. I took pictures—which darned near got me kicked out of Calvary, let me tell you. Amanda also sent me a questionnaire to fill out about the minister, the demographics of the congregation, and a bunch of other stuff."

Lottie dug a stapled bunch of papers out of her purse and handed it to me.

"She wants to know what the church smells like?" I asked as I read down the questions. "Do they have incense in Baptist churches? Is that what she means?"

"No, she wants to know the smell. Is it musty or does it have an antiseptic odor? Floral? Lemony furniture wax? She also was very particular about the minister's breath, which was kind of unfair if you ask me. Just because the guy popped a mint before his Sunday Sermon doesn't mean he's not going to smell of last night's garlic before the wedding."

"Wait. I thought the wedding was in Atlanta where Amanda lives? Or possibly on some Caribbean island?"

Lottie plopped down on one of the porch chairs. "Now she wants to have it here. Honestly, it's a lot easier on Scotty and me if she has it here. And I'm secretly thrilled to have her married in her home town."

I sat down beside Lottie, still confused. "But you put a deposit down on a reception hall in Atlanta and it's non-refundable!"

We'd spoken about this last month when Amanda had suddenly decided she might want a destination wedding. And *two* dresses. I'd assumed that Lottie and her husband were going to hold firm to their budget and have a tough-love talk with their daughter, but clearly that hadn't happened.

"I was able to get half the deposit back from the hall in Atlanta." Lottie grimaced. "I know, I know. At least I managed to talk her out of an island wedding and the two gowns. I figured this was a good compromise."

A good compromise would have been Amanda getting married in Atlanta, like she'd planned, since her parents had already shelled out money for the venue, but what was done was done. Me being outraged wouldn't help when Lottie clearly needed my support right now.

"It *will* be easier to organize things here instead of flying down to Atlanta every month," I agreed. "And I'm guessing most of her family and school friends are here as well."

Lottie nodded. "They are, although her college friends and her work colleagues will need to fly up. Plus all of her fiancé's family as well. And it's going to be hard to find a church and a venue in the area that will accommodate her guest list. These things are so much easier to arrange in a larger city. There's only one florist in Reckless, and I know she's going to be picky about the caterer. No Chat-n-Chew for Amanda. Which is a darned shame. They've got that shrimp wrapped in bacon which is perfect for wedding receptions in my opinion."

Shrimp wrapped in bacon sounded good to me. I saw what Lottie meant though. If Amanda wanted award-winning floral displays and fusion cuisine, then she was better off getting married in Atlanta.

"Has she changed the date?" I wondered, thinking they'd have even less time to plan if Amanda still wanted her wedding this October.

"No." Lottie chewed her lip. "That's one of the good things about having it local, though. In Atlanta, all the best sites get booked up a year in advance. We might not have fancy hotels with marble and gold, but at least you can reserve the Legion Hall with only a few months' notice."

I watched my friend's expression carefully. "And Amanda will be happy with the Legion Hall? And Reckless Reformed Baptist? And the bacon-wrapped shrimp from the Chat-n-Chew catering? Or do you think she'll change her mind again?"

Lottie sighed, then rubbed her forehead before replying. "I don't know. I insisted she come up next month and see everything for herself before I put another dollar down in deposit." She turned to face me. "I don't know what's going on with her, Sassy. At first I thought it was just the excitement of her wedding, then I thought she was getting these unrealistic ideas from social media and those reality shows, but something's wrong. Scotty and I always spoiled Amanda, but she's never been this bad. Never."

I thought for a second. "Is there trouble in paradise? Maybe she and Eric have hit a rocky patch and she's having second thoughts?"

Lottie pursed her lips. "I did think about that. Maybe she's turned into a bridezilla as a way to eventually call the wedding off? Eric has just gone along with everything so far. He pretty much is letting her plan the whole thing without any input from him or his family, so if her goal is to irritate him enough that he calls it off, I think she's driving down the wrong road."

"Perhaps the problem is his lack of involvement," I suggested. "Some women want total control over their wedding plans, but others truly want it to be something the both of them plan together. Could Amanda want Eric to be more involved, and her wild ideas and the constant changes and indecision are a way to force him to take a more active role?"

"Maybe." Lottie shrugged. "Amanda isn't shy about taking charge, but I remember when she was a teen that she was happier when her friends all joined in on the planning. But Eric is Eric. She agreed to marry him as he is, and wanting him to change and suddenly be driving around to florists with her, weighing in on zinnias versus roses isn't realistic. You can't change a person. You marry who they are, not who you think they could be with some work on your part."

Very wise words, although I didn't like the slightly bitter tone with which Lottie had delivered them.

I reached out to pat her shoulder. "Let's go inside. Elvis deserves a treat, and we do too. Coffee and a muffin from the day-old basket?"

Elvis jumped to his feet, his tail wagging furiously at the word "treat."

Lottie smiled over at me, then stood as well. "It's a date."

Lottie and I went inside, selected our muffins, and sat at the little café table, Elvis gnawing on a peanut-butter stuffed Kong that I'd pulled out of the back freezer for him.

"Gossip time," Lottie announced before taking a bite of her lemon zest muffin.

"About the dead body Elvis found in the woods yesterday?"

She nodded. "Rumor has it that the remains are—"

"Buddy Hooper's." I laughed at her surprised expression. "Jake was here earlier. He said the town gossip mill is saying it's Buddy's body."

"And is Jake confirming the gossip?" Lottie leaned forward in excitement.

"Uh, no. In fact, Jake tried to dispel those rumors. He said they're hoping the DNA gets a match and they can identify the man that way, but that there's no evidence that the remains are Buddy Hooper's."

"But Buddy went missing last June or July," Lottie sputtered. "And sources that know say Steff is putting the body's time of death between May and August last year. That can't be a coincidence. Reckless isn't a big town. If a missing person and a dead body overlap on a timeline, it makes sense to think they're the same person."

I held up my hands at Lottie's argument. "I know, but Jake said Buddy had a lot of debt and that he was being evicted. He said most missing adults are missing voluntarily, and that there was no indication that Buddy was doing anything but skipping out on his financial obligations to start fresh somewhere else. Plus, Reckless might be a small town, but we get a lot of tourists *and* we get a lot of hikers. It seems like a weird coincidence, I know, but this body is probably not Buddy's."

Lottie scowled. "I respect Jake. He's a professional and he knows what he's doing, but he's looking at all of this like a cop. I'm looking at this like a citizen of Reckless who grew up in the town, as someone who knows the people who live here. *I* think there's more than a good chance the body is Buddy's."

I took a sip of my coffee and thought about that. Lottie *did* know the town and the people here, but I was on Jake's side of the fence on this one. Still, a man had gone missing, and even though Jake seemed to think that was because he wanted to go missing, it still didn't sit right with me. Surely someone would have known that Buddy Hooper was going to take off like that. Wouldn't he have cleared out his belongings? Hired a moving truck or a storage unit? Sold off equipment or supplies for cash to start new somewhere else? The sheriff's department hadn't really looked into his disappearance, but a quick check of his credit report could reveal if he was living and working in another state. Even if he had a cash-under-the-table job, nobody could sniff out a missing person like the skip tracers that lenders hired to find those who owed them money.

And as worried as I was about Mom's weird white-hat hacking hobby, it might come in handy here.

"The police aren't going to tie this to Buddy's disappearance unless there's substantial evidence." I waited for Lottie's nod before continuing. "Maybe Buddy did leave voluntarily. Maybe he didn't. There's nothing stopping us from looking into his disappearance, though."

Lottie nodded enthusiastically. "If we ask around, dig into some stuff, and find he's living in North Carolina or something, then no harm done."

"And if we find out he's truly vanished, and that there's evidence of foul play…"

"Then we can take it to the sheriff's office, and they can pursue it further," Lottie finished. "And maybe we'll find enough to connect Buddy to this body Elvis found as well."

"We'll be helping to solve a murder," I said. "Or at least, a missing persons case from last year."

Lottie grinned. "Then let's do it. Let's find Buddy Hooper."

I nodded. "First, I need to know everything about the guy. He was gone before I even bought the campground, so I never met him."

Lottie blew out a breath and leaned back in her chair. "Buddy moved here about ten years ago and started work as a farm hand for Marcie Boarding's husband, Jason. After a few years, Jason found out that Buddy was leasing farmland and doing side work, but using Jason's equipment."

I shook my head, thinking that sounded like the sort of thing the man Jake described would do.

"There was quite a fight, and Jason ended up firing Buddy. Buddy bought some equipment of his own on credit, rented a farm and leased additional land. Basically he farmed leased land—mostly hay fields, and sold the hay. He also hauled for people—stuff like heavy equipment deliveries and moving tractors across the county. He was doing well, but with Buddy, cash flow was always a serious problem."

"Jake had said that Buddy wasn't very good with money," I commented.

"I don't want to completely blame Buddy. He had payments on the equipment he'd bought. He had his rent costs for the farm plus the costs for all the leased land. People complained all the time that he was shorting bales and calling hay second cut that wasn't. Yeah, Buddy was sneaky when it came to that stuff, but I think a lot of that was him trying to make ends meet." Lottie wrinkled her nose. "Not that money problems are a reason to rip people off."

"Maybe his debts just got too much for him," I mused, thinking that Buddy probably *was* somewhere in North Carolina working for another farm and trying to recover from his business failings.

"Possibly," Lottie said. "Everyone in town knew Buddy was overextended, but he was the kind of guy to take those risks. In my opinion, it was a flip of the coin whether he'd make a profit on all his businesses or go under."

"You realize that all this is supporting Jake's belief that the guy took off to avoid his debts," I pointed out.

"I know. And I know that it's reasonable for someone to do that when they were in over their head like Buddy was, but I don't believe it," Lottie said. "I think he would have stuck it out to the bitter end. He would have come up with twenty different schemes to get himself out of financial trouble, and kept at it. He wouldn't have just given up and taken off when things weren't really dire."

"Lottie, he was being evicted from the farm he was renting," I pointed out. "That sounds pretty dire to me."

Lottie waved a hand. "It wasn't the first time Buddy was on the edge of eviction. He always managed to find the money at the last minute."

I tried to keep my skepticism in check and remain open-minded, but I was thinking this might have been the one time Buddy couldn't find the money at the last minute, and took off rather than face a notice taped to his front door.

"When Buddy went missing last summer, no one realized it for a month or so. There were complaints about hay deliveries not being met in mid-June, and a few people wondered about not seeing him around town, but no one reported him missing right away," Lottie added.

I shook my head. "That's really sad. Jake told me that Buddy wasn't always honest in his dealings, but it's heartbreaking that someone could vanish for a month and no one was close enough to him to worry or even care. I can't believe he didn't have any family, friends, or a serious girlfriend."

"Buddy was a bit of a ladies' man, but I got the impression he wasn't one for any sort of regular relationship. A girlfriend surely would have noticed him not returning calls and suddenly not showing up." Lottie shrugged. "Or maybe not. He was probably one of those guys who cancelled a date by text, and would go weeks without returning calls or contacting someone."

"Jake said the everyone just assumed Buddy took off before he got evicted," I told Lottie. "Jake also said that Buddy made a habit of not paying bills or rent until they were so overdue he was facing legal action. That's why they didn't think his disappearance involved foul play even after he was being evicted from the farm."

Lottie made a "tsk" noise. "It's a pain in the butt to evict someone. You have to haul yourself down to the courthouse in Derwood and file the paperwork, then wait two or three weeks for a court date. When you show up in court, it's still not over. The judge basically says 'yes, the tenant owes the money' then gives them another two weeks to pay it. If they pay, you're still out the time and money for the filing, and there's nothing stopping them from not paying the following month. Then you have to do it all over again."

"And if they don't pay in the two weeks the judge gave them?" I asked.

"Then you have to go *back* to the courthouse and fill out more papers. There's a second hearing, and if they still haven't paid, you're awarded the eviction. But the fun continues, because the Sheriff's office needs to hang a notice on the tenant's door giving them a week or two to move all their stuff out and announcing an actual eviction date. You and I both know how short staffed the Sheriff's office is around here, so it takes them a while to deliver the notice."

I grunted in sympathy.

"On eviction day, a deputy shows up and you both knock on the tenant's door," Lottie continued. "Usually they're gone by then. If they're not, the deputy escorts them off the premises while you change the locks. Most of the time the house still has a bunch of their stuff in it. You can't get rid of the stuff, you've got to put it out on the curb for twenty-four hours to give the tenant another chance to gather it up. So you pay a crew to haul the stuff to the curb, then pay them to come back the next day and haul whatever hasn't been picked up or stolen to the dump. If you don't haul the stuff off in the next day, the city fines you for having trash outside your property."

"Sounds like you have some past experience in evictions," I commented.

"Scotty and I rented out my parents' house for a year after mom died. Let's just say that after a year, we fixed up the house and sold it."

I knew there were plenty of slumlords around, and I had mixed feelings about the whole property rental business, but at the end of the day, people needed a place to stay and lots of those people couldn't buy, weren't ready to buy, or didn't want to buy. They needed safe, clean, well-maintained rental options at reasonable prices. Landlords also needed to know their properties weren't going to be trashed and that they were going to get the agreed upon rent.

"I don't think I could ever manage a rental property," I told Lottie. "Managing the campground is hard enough. At least my guests don't stay more than a few weeks—except for Mickey Morse that is. She stayed for almost a month. And at least I've never had to kick anyone out."

Although I *had* worried about it when those rowdy Mason brothers had been here.

"It's not fun," she agreed. "Although from what I heard, Buddy Hooper wasn't a terrible tenant. He always paid late, but Tony said he kept the place in good shape, and managed the hay fields well. No thistles or briars or anything."

"You know Buddy Hooper's landlord?" I asked.

Of course she did. Lottie knew pretty much everyone in Reckless and the surrounding areas.

"Tony Marconi." She grinned. "I went to school with him. He's a good guy. His father was a property developer who liked to buy up distressed properties and farms. Sometimes he'd rent them, sometimes he'd fix them up and flip them, sometimes he'd just sit on the land and wait for the right political climate to get the zoning and permits for a development. Tony went into the family business and took over when his father died about twenty years ago."

I took a sip of my coffee. "I wonder if Tony remembers anything about Buddy going missing. He must have had some idea of when the farmhouse was unoccupied, or if there was anything unusual about the stuff he put on the curb."

"Maybe I should give him a call," Lottie said.

"That would be awesome. It would be great if your old school friend had a few leads we could use to track down where Buddy went, and find out if he's still alive or not.

"We'll probably need more than whatever clues Tony can provide," Lottie commented. "I wonder if there's a way to put a trace on Buddy's cell phone, or his truck license, or his banking stuff? It's almost impossible to completely go off grid nowadays. If Buddy moved elsewhere, he would have continued to use his debit card and his phone."

"I don't think we can put a trace on his phone or license plate, but I'm willing to bet we can check his credit report and see if there's been any activity in the last year," I told Lottie.

"Your mom?" Lottie grinned.

"My mom," I agreed. "But no one knows about that. I don't want her getting into trouble." Especially I was pretty sure a lot of what she was doing over the internet was downright illegal.

Lottie made a "lips sealed" motion, throwing away the imaginary key. We sipped our coffee and thought in silence for a few moments until Lottie finally spoke up.

"It could take Stef weeks to get anything from the DNA," Lottie informed me. "Weeks. Maybe even months. And in the meantime, the investigation will be on hold because they don't want to spend valuable time and resources potentially on the wrong guy. It's not like a recent murder where you've only got the first forty-eight hours to solve it before your chance of success plummets. This thing is already a cold case. Stef said the remains were there at least a year."

"What are you saying?" I knew exactly what Lottie was saying, but I still wanted her to put it out there verbally.

"I'm saying we *do* need to investigate this."

"I'm in." I told Lottie without the slightest hesitation. "What should we do first? The credit search or talk to his former landlord?"

"Talk to Tony," she said. "I'll call him and get him to meet us tomorrow afternoon for lunch at The Coffee Dog. Does that work for you? I know things are slower on Mondays so hopefully you can get away."

"I can slip out for a few hours." Mom always came in at ten to take over the store, and I doubted I'd be needed until later in the day.

"Then I'll set things up." Lottie took out her phone and typed something in. "I also want to run by Reckless Self Storage. If Buddy wanted to bail and leave town because of the eviction, he would have moved his stuff somewhere safe until he had a new address. He might have rented a storage unit for June of last year. And if he picked up all the stuff in a moving truck after that, we'll know he intended to ditch town and move somewhere else."

I thought about that a second. "He could have rented a storage unit, or decided to just leave everything behind except for clothes and some memorabilia. If he was hard up for cash, he might have just abandoned his property."

Lottie nodded. "Tony should be able to tell us what was left in the farmhouse when he had to put it all on the curb. I'm still thinking Buddy might have rented a storage unit, though. It's expensive to replace furniture and stuff, and it's a whole lot cheaper to rent a place for a month or two to store it until you've got a lease on a new place."

"Maybe he asked a friend to keep it for him," I pointed out.

"True, but I'm pretty sure that friend would have come forward sometime in the last year and said 'Buddy's not dead. He showed up last week to get his sofa.' Or 'Hey. This guy's missing and I'm tired of his junk in my garage.'"

I nodded in agreement. "But if Buddy put his belongings all in storage, he might have been using a facility outside of Reckless."

"I'm willing to bet he would have stored it locally until he figured out where he was moving to," Lottie said. "There's no sense in driving an hour back and forth with truckloads of stuff, when you can move it all three or four miles down the road."

"True." I thought for a second. "If he never showed up to empty the unit, then I'm sure they've sold his stuff after all this time. From what Jake said, Buddy doesn't strike me as the type to pay a year up front for a storage unit."

"True, but I think it's worth looking into." Lottie stood up, draining her coffee and gathering her trash. "I'll pick you up at eleven tomorrow?"

"I'll be ready," I told her.

CHAPTER 7

The old Mercedes sedan pulled down the drive at eight o'clock. I was relaxing on the sofa watching dog tracking videos on YouTube when Elvis alerted me that someone was pulling up in front of the house. I peeked out the window, saw the car, then went back to the sofa, not wanting to look like I was spying on Mom and her friend.

"I'm back," she announced as she came through the door. "And I'm stuffed. Rosalind and I had lunch at The Coffee Dog after the knitting club, then went antique shopping in Savage. We ate dinner at a Korean place just outside of town. I had my doubts but it was amazing. Best kimchee I've had in years. The waitress said the owner makes it herself—none of that stuff in a jar. Rosalind had barbeque, but I had the bibimbap, and it was amazing. We have to go sometime, Sassy."

She sounded so excited, so lively. It was contagious and I found myself sitting up, putting my laptop aside and listening to her describe her day. I was so glad she'd taken the whole day off and enjoyed herself without any worry about me or the campground. I was so glad she'd found a friend.

"How about you? How was your day?" she asked once I'd heard all about the knitting projects, the brass spittoon that Rosalind had decided she needed to have, and the red bean paste ice cream they'd both had for dessert.

"I had a relaxing day. Elvis and I did some search and rescue training with the twins. I discovered that there is a hole in the side of the speedboat and the motor is missing from the pontoon boat."

"Oh no! Can we pick up a used one somewhere? How much do they cost? Should we go online and see if anyone has a motor for sale?" Mom asked.

I waved a hand. "I'll look later. And Jake is going to keep his eye out for one. He also updated me about the body Elvis found, and Lottie came by later to discuss it as well. We're going to see if we can track down a guy who went missing last year about the time Stef thinks the man in the woods might have died. The police didn't do much to look for him, since they had reason to believe he'd skipped town to run out on some debts. Oh—and Lottie's daughter now wants to have her wedding here in Reckless! Lottie seems happy about it, in spite of the extra work. I think she just wants Amanda home for her big day instead of having the wedding in Atlanta. Or in the islands."

"I can understand that. It's so nice when the kids come home for their special events," Mom commented. "I hope we get invitations. I didn't think we'd be able to swing going to Atlanta at the tail end of our season, but I'm sure we can take a day off if the wedding is local."

Lottie hadn't said anything about our being on the guest list, but I intended on sending a gift anyway. Plus if the wedding was local, I might be able to help out in some way.

"So, tell me about this missing man," Mom continued. "Why don't the police think the remains are his?"

"It's not that they're totally ruling that out," I explained.

"Jake says they just don't want to focus the investigation in that direction only to find out that the missing guy has been living and working in North Carolina for a year, and the body belonged to a hiker."

"That makes sense. But Lottie is convinced it's him?" Mom asked.

I wiggled my hand. "It's more like the whole town thinks it's him. Lottie thinks if we employ our amateur sleuthing to finding the missing man, we'll either have solid information to give the police, or be able to put the rumors to rest."

Mom set her purse on the table, plopped down on the sofa, and slid her laptop over. "The easiest way to find a missing person is the internet. Social media. Parking tickets. Credit reports. If he's alive he's used a cell phone, or charged gas, leased an apartment, or signed up for utilities."

I loved how I didn't even need to ask Mom to help dig up information for me. "According to Lottie he lived her in Reckless for ten years. He did farm labor when he first arrived, but quickly branched out into his own farming, leasing land and even renting a farm to live at. Supposedly he wasn't very good with money, and he was in the process of being evicted when he disappeared."

"What information do you have on him?" Mom asked. "Full name? Social security number? Last known address? Birthdate?"

Well, darn. Maybe this wouldn't be as easy as I'd thought. "I think he's in his midthirties, but I don't know his birthdate or even his birth year. Or his address. Or his middle name." I grimaced. "Actually, I'm not sure his first name is really Buddy or if that's a nickname. All I know is Buddy Hooper, Reckless Virginia."

Mom sighed.

"I can get more information tomorrow," I assured her. "Lottie has to know his full name and we're meeting his former landlord, so I can get his address. And the landlord might know his date of birth from the application or something."

"Let's see what I can find with the information you've got." Mom started typing. "Judicial case records are public and searchable. I'll put in his last name, sort by county, and see what's on there. If he went to court for a speeding ticket or anything else, there's bound to be a record of it. From there I might be able to get his legal name as well as the month and year of his birth."

I crossed my fingers and waited while Mom typed away. From what Lottie and Jake had said, Buddy had scammed a lot of people. But it seems like those scams had been small stuff that might not have resulted in any sort of civil suit. It was more likely that he would have had a traffic ticket he'd gone to court over. Although there might have been lots of people with the last name Hooper who disputed traffic tickets in the state.

"Here's an Eric Hooper that got pulled over in Derwood for speeding." Mom peered at the screen. "There's no date of birth on the listing, and no address. Then there's a Raymond Hooper with a child support filing, a Sylvester Hooper with a wage garnishment. Five 'B' Hoopers with different charges, some of them in this area."

I sighed. "Well, it was worth a shot. Thanks for trying, Mom."

"Get me his full legal name, an address, and a date of birth and I'll see what I can pull up," she told me. "If you can also get me his social security number, driver's license number, make and model of his car and his license plate information, then I can probably find a whole lot more. At the very least, his credit report should show if he's taken out any loans for new farming equipment. It'll also show if his credit cards are in default or if he's been paying them this past year. There might be a speeding ticket in another state this past year that would prove he's either still alive, or that someone stole his license as well as his truck and is driving it around."

It wasn't any real emergency, but I texted Lottie, hoping she'd know the information Mom needed. Then I did some internet research of my own, checking out GPS collars for Elvis. He already had the nice leather one I used for his leash, and an electronic collar that vibrated to alert him that he needed to stop sniffing and pay attention to what I was saying—which was usually my yelling for him to come to me. When we were tracking, I generally swapped out his leather collar for a brightly colored nylon harness, and left off the e-collar since many clubs and events didn't allow them. But the Reckless Sniffers clearly allowed a GPS collar, and given that I'd already had several panicked moments when I was afraid I'd lost my hound, getting one definitely sounded like a good idea.

"Oof," I muttered as the first collar I'd pulled up was nearly fifteen hundred dollars. I scrolled, then pulled up a few that were more in my price range.

One supposedly also monitored health stats including hours sleeping, food intake, and exercise. I wasn't looking for the canine equivalent of a FitBit, so I bypassed that one and also bypassed one that required a hefty monthly subscription. A few articles suggested putting an Apple or Tile tag on your dog's collar, like they were checked luggage at the airport, but neither of those seemed to have the range or the durability I was looking for. Others were basically invisible fence collars with alerts that pinged your phone if your dog got out, and provided limited information on where they'd wandered to, but that wasn't really what I wanted either.

I kept searching, knowing there must be something specifically created for sporting and hunting dogs that were frequently off leash and might be more likely to get lost than the typical dog.

Finally I landed on the Rio Grande Electronics website, remembering that Andy had mentioned the club members had gotten their collars through there because Mike Allen had been able to give them a discount. I didn't feel like I knew Mike well enough to call him up and request a discount of my own, but as I scrolled through the listings, it was clear that Rio Grande really did have the best prices. And you couldn't beat the free shipping and delivery time. They had warehouses all over the area, so anything I ordered would be here in two days at most.

I finally settled on a Garmin brand GPS collar. It looked a little silly with the antennae sprouting from the collar, but the description said the wire provided a more accurate location as well as the ability to detect the dog at greater distances from the handheld device. Prices ranged from two to seven hundred, which was certainly better than the fifteen-hundred dollar one I'd first seen, but significantly more than just slapping an Apple Air Tag on Elvis.

I looked up at the blue tarp that was *still* covering the hole in my ceiling. I had hoped to attempt a repair this week, but in order to do that, I'd need to run in to the home improvement store in Derwood and pick up a sheet of drywall, a bucket of spackle, and some drywall tape. I'd watched several YouTube videos, and had pulled the needed tools out of the garage. All that remained was to purchase the supplies, set up a ladder, and hope for the best. However badly my repair went, it had to look better than a blue tarp.

I'd estimated a hundred dollars in materials—a hundred dollars that could go to Elvis's GPS collar. My finger hovered over the button to put the collar into the cart, but I hesitated. Was this just me, trying to delay doing a repair that unnerved me far more than the washing machine issue last month? I tried to argue that Elvis's safety came first, but his safety could be achieved by just keeping him on a leash or making sure his vibration collar was on.

Images ran through my mind, memories of Elvis yanking the leash out of my hand and racing into the woods. I'd been so afraid, fearing that the worst might happen to my buddy. That was the deciding factor as I put the collar into my shopping cart, and completed the transaction.

The hole in the ceiling would just need to wait for another month. Elvis was more important.

My phone beeped just as I'd gotten the online receipt for my GPS collar purchase. It was Lottie, returning my text.

I turned to Mom. "Do you want to try again on that case search information?"

"Absolutely." She put her book aside and pulled her laptop toward her. "Go ahead."

"Buddy Hooper's real name is Harvey Hooper." I grimaced, thinking that I'd prefer to be called Buddy as well. Harvey Hooper? Who would do that to a kid? "Lottie doesn't have his exact date of birth, but she's sure he turned 35 last year." I read off the address to the farm that Buddy had been renting from Tony, adding that Lottie thought he might have originally been from somewhere in the panhandle of Florida.

Mom typed away, finally looking up at me. "The only thing I found in the case search was a civil case from five years ago. It seems Buddy kept his nose clean as far as the law went—not even any unpaid parking tickets or traffic violations. The civil case was between him and a Marcus LaSalle. Buddy was the defendant."

"Marcus?" I frowned. "He's with the Reckless Sniffers Club. I met him on Saturday. He's got a bloodhound as well, but his is a fancy pedigreed show dog."

"You don't need any fancy pedigree, Elvis," Mom said to

the hound sleeping by her feet. "We love you even if you don't have papers."

I would never criticize people who bought their dogs from reputable breeders—breeders who did genetic testing, had contracts where they would take the dog back at any time for any reason, and cared deeply about the future of the breed and the well-being of the dogs they brought into the world. It was puppy mills and careless breeders trying to make a fast buck who were the cause of all the dogs in shelters and rescues. But I hadn't been looking for a hunting dog or a show dog when I'd set out to adopt. I'd wanted a companion, one who would keep me active but not be too high-energy. I'd wanted a dog who would be friendly and outgoing with strangers. I'd wanted an adult dog, and wasn't worried about their exact age.

There had been so many dogs needing a forever family, but the moment I'd seen Elvis, I'd fallen in love. There had been something about his soulful dark eyes, his saggy jowls and wrinkled forehead that tugged at my heart. The rescue was in Texas. I'd put in an application, submitted references, did an interview, and two weeks later, my new best friend had walked through my door.

And had promptly shook his head, sending long strands of drool flying onto my walls and ceiling. Elvis slobbered. His snoring was louder than a circular saw. His flatulence should be registered as a biological weapon. He liked to roll in stinky stuff, and he counter surfed, eating anything we accidently left out. I'd had to put locks on cabinets and on the garbage can, and put baby gates up through the house after he'd eaten a box of Cheerios from the cabinet, a container of two-week-old spaghetti that I'd thrown out, and two banana nut loaves cooling on the stove top. He didn't always come when he was called. He hogged the bed. He figured out how to open doors, resulting in my putting dead-bolt locks on all the exterior doors of my house.

I wouldn't trade him for anything. I wouldn't trade him for Marcus's fancy-pants bloodhound, Nose.

"Looks like it was settled out of court," Mom said, pulling my attention back to the search for information on Buddy Hooper. "It had something to do with an unfulfilled contract and maybe fraud?"

"Jake said that Buddy had a habit of misrepresenting his hay and even shorting bales," I told her. "Maybe Marcus decided to be the one to do something about it."

"Maybe." Mom shrugged. "Even though they settled before it went before the judge, you still might want to dig around and find out the details of what happened. It could be that Marcus was still holding a grudge."

I made a quick note to ask Lottie if she either knew what happened or if she could dig around and find out the details of the lawsuit.

"His credit report is a darned mess, but I think we kind of expected that," Mom said, typing once more. "There was a whole lot of late payments on stuff going back years. Looks like he paid off his truck and his tractor spring of last year, though."

"What?" I got up and went over to sit beside Mom to look at the report.

"Here." She pointed at the screen. "And here."

I stared at the data, not sure if I understood what I was looking at. "He was being evicted. He was in desperate straits financially. Are you sure you're reading it right? How could he have the money to pay off a truck and a tractor, and not have the money for his rent?"

"Last balance on the truck was six thousand two hundred, so it's not like he owed fifty grand on it or anything," Mom said. "The tractor had a balance of twelve grand, so that's a bit more. Maybe he put all his cash toward paying off the more important things, and stiffed his landlord because he knew he was leaving town?"

I frowned, wondering if that was the case. Buddy was clearly an unscrupulous person. If he had a job offer elsewhere, and knew he'd be leaving town in June or July, perhaps he had prioritized paying off his truck over rent. But his tractor? Had he taken the tractor with him when he'd gone? Did this hypothetical new job even require him to own a tractor? I could absolutely see someone paying off the loan on their vehicle if they wanted to start fresh, but the tractor seemed...odd.

"He didn't have any credit cards," Mom commented. "At least, none that hadn't been closed years ago. I'm willing to bet no one offered him a credit card in the last two years. He definitely wasn't good at paying his bills, and he does have a bunch of accounts that are in collection."

I stared at the screen. "But are they in collection because he vanished a year ago?"

"They were in collection before that." Mom turned to face me. "There's nothing in this credit report that sets off any alarms, in my opinion. He doesn't have any new accounts established in the last year, but given his credit report, I can't imagine that anyone would give him a loan on anything. He's a deadbeat credit-wise, but he's always been a deadbeat. It's not like someone who always paid every bill on time suddenly stopped paying and went into collection. He's always not paid, or waited until he was on the steps of the courthouse before he paid. There's nothing surprising here. Maybe he was killed last summer. Or maybe he ghosted on all these debts and is living in another state."

"But he paid off his truck. And the tractor." I frowned once more.

"He did." Mom closed the browser tab and set her laptop

aside. "Lots of folks who have debt and credit problems live a cash life and just let the financial institutions write off their losses. Some people have no choice. And some people just have different priorities."

Part of me wanted to judge Buddy for his lousy payment history, but I knew nothing about his life. Glancing once more at the tarp on my ceiling, I realized that to judge him would put me dangerously near to being a hypocrite. I was cutting it close financially with the purchase of the camp-ground and my expenditures. I was one disaster away from missing bills myself. When I'd gotten cancer, I'd been lucky that I'd not only had good insurance through my job, but I'd also had short-term disability and a large bank of saved vacation and sick leave. Not everyone had that privilege.

I didn't have that privilege now. That great corporate insurance was gone, and I was paying through the nose for an individual plan until I was old enough for Medicare. Thank the Lord for the laws that made it possible for me to have an insurance plan. A few decades ago, I would have been denied coverage, and have been forced to stay in my corporate job just to be insured.

But Buddy wasn't a cancer survivor in his late fifties, pinching pennies and trying to make a new business venture work. He'd somehow made enough to pay off eighteen grand of debt while ignoring his rent and other bills. We weren't the same. And I was totally going to judge him.

CHAPTER 8

*L*ottie picked me up promptly at ten forty-five Monday morning. I'd been up at five like usual, and had been able to squeeze in a little hide-and-seek practice with Elvis and the twins after Mom had arrived at ten to take over manning the camp store. We parked down the block and walked up to The Coffee Dog right at eleven, but Tony had gotten there early.

I don't know what I expected, but the good-looking fifty-something guy in jeans and a well-worn olive-green T-shirt wasn't what I'd been envisioning when Lottie scheduled this meeting with Tony Marconi.

The developer already had a table and a coffee. He stood when we approached and came around the table to give Lottie a hug.

"It's been a few years, Lottie-pop." He kissed the side of her head and hugged her tighter.

His voice surprised me as well. He had a soft, southern Virginia drawl when I'd been imagining New Jersey Italian.

"Tony Marconi." Lottie let the hug go on a second longer

then pulled away and swatted the man on the arm. "Now, that's enough. I'm a married woman, you know."

"Oh, I know." He sighed and dramatically clutched his chest. "How is Scotty, that lucky man. And the kids? Good grief, Amanda probably has kids of her own by now, and Aaron? Is he still in college?"

Lottie laughed, a high-pitched sound that told me how flustered she was. "I don't have any grandkids yet. Amanda is working in Atlanta. She's engaged. The wedding is this fall. Aaron graduates next year. He's majoring in history, though, so I expect him to ask us to help with grad school. We'd assumed he would go into teaching at the high-school level, but he's been making noises about becoming a professor."

I noticed she didn't say anything about how Scotty was.

The smile Tony gave Lottie filled with admiration. "That's amazing. I hope I get a wedding invitation, Lottie-pop. Who's your friend?"

"Oh. Oh!" Lottie turned to me with an apologetic smile. "This is Sassy Letouroux. She and her mother bought the Reckless Camper Campground."

"Nice to meet you, Miss Sassy." Tony shook my hand. "I was eyeing the campground after Len Trout died, but unfortunately all my cash was tied up with another development in Derwood and a strip mall we're building over in Peabody Heights. If the old man had hung on another year, I might have out bid you." He wiggled a finger at me, a smile on his face.

"Well then, it was good for me that you were having a cash flow issue," I told him, shuddering at the thought of the developer buying the campground. I doubt he would have run the business as it was. Tony probably would have torn down all the cabins and put up condos or something.

"Did you all see my Swallows Landing development on the Savage side of the lake?" Tony asked, digging his phone out of his pocket. "This is what I would have done with the campground if I'd a had the cash to handle an extra project."

Lottie and I leaned close to Tony while he swiped though pictures and talked enthusiastically about the development. From the photos it looked like it was nearly finished, and almost half the homes looked to be already occupied. There was a set of condos near the entrance to the development, then several blocks of townhomes, but the lake-view and lakefront lots were filled with what would be sprawling luxury homes when they were finished. It was pretty. And I was very thankful that this hadn't been the campground's fate.

"We're getting ready to put in the beach area now," Tony said, showing more pictures of large construction equipment both digging and filling in sections of lake front. "Once we finish and get the sand in, we'll be done and those lakefront houses will be ready for their buyers. Sassy, if you don't mind, I'd like to drop by in the next day or two and take a look at your lakefront beach. I know Len Trout did a nice job there, and I'd like the one in this development to be similar."

"Sure. Just come on by." I had no idea what he was actually expecting to get out of that visit. From what I could tell, it was just a whole bunch of sand dumped in front of and in the lake. The sand went about ten feet into the water, and the beach area was approximately a hundred feet long and fifty feet wide. Maybe there was some engineering and planning that had gone into the whole thing, but from my point of view, it was just sand.

Lottie pointed to one of the pictures on Tony's phone. "That's the section of the lake that had the big drop-off, right? I remember us going out there as kids. We had a swing that went out over the lake, and you could climb up on a big rock and dive off into the water. It was really deep there."

Tony nodded. "Yep. It took a lot of grading to make the

beach a gradual slope instead of that huge drop. All those trees had to come out—big rocks as well."

I had to blink back tears at that. A childhood swimming spot gone. A tree swing and a diving rock gone. Everything ripped up and smoothed over for houses and a sandy beach. People needed to live somewhere, and I of all people understood the appeal of the lake, but it still hurt to hear about natural areas being razed and flattened

"The job won't stop at the waterline," Tony continued. "There needed to be a gradual slope in the lake as well so little kids can wade in without suddenly plunging into ten or twenty feet of water. Pretty much all the dirt we took from the beach area is going into the lake to provide a safer swimming area. We were schedule to add the fill-dirt today, but we were halted until some guy from the state goes in the water with a wetsuit and a metal detector. Time is money, and we're already a little behind schedule with this development, so I'm hoping he finishes by the end of the week and we can get back to work."

I frowned, puzzled as to why someone from the state needed to swim around with a metal detector before Tony could proceed. "What is he looking for? This guy with the metal detector, I mean."

Tony shrugged. "There's some other electronics he's using too. I think he's just making sure we're not burying anything historical before it gets photographed and documented. Kinda crazy, given that everything pretty much got buried when they flooded the valley for the lake a hundred years ago."

"There are structures down on the lake bottom," Lottie explained. "People lived and farmed the valley before they put the lake in. Most of it's probably rotted or buried under silt at this point, but it *is* an interesting part of the lake's history that needs to be documented."

"So this man will search for signs of stone foundations or farming tools or stuff like that?"

Lottie nodded. "He'll take photos, document the locations, and then Tony can continue. They're not trying to excavate anything. They want to fill in the information gaps in the documents that remain from when the valley was flooded. For historical reasons."

I could appreciate that since I was planning on doing a lake cruise that focused on the area's history.

"Are you all getting coffee and lunch, or is there a party on the sidewalk that I wasn't invited to?" I turned to see Sierra with her head poked out of The Coffee Dog's front door.

"I'll be inside in a second to order. We're just catching up with Tony," Lottie told her. "But you're welcome to join us."

"I wish I could but I'm solo here today and have a ton of phone orders to get through." Sierra walked out of The Coffee Dog toward our table. "Why don't I just grab your orders now. You all can sit, chat, and I'll bring everything out when it's ready."

She pulled a pen and an order pad out of her back pocket and eyed us expectantly. We all ordered Reubens and drinks. Once Sierra had brought out our coffees the three of us sat.

"I actually called you because I wanted to ask some questions about Buddy Hooper," Lottie said to Tony.

He clutched his chest again. "What? It wasn't my charm and good looks that you were after, but information on a tenant I had to evict last year? I'm crushed, Lottie. Crushed."

He wasn't wrong about the charm and good looks, although the intense flirting made me a bit uncomfortable. Still, Tony was a very attractive man, fit with a dark tan, thick silver hair, and warm brown eyes. He had a dimple in his strong chin, and high cheekbones. The lines at the corner of his eyes and bracketing his mouth only added to his appeal. But the fact that he was well aware of his attractiveness and was clearly working it, kind of ruined the appeal for me.

"Yes, because I'm *married*," Lottie said with a slight giggle. "Now, what can you tell us about Buddy? Was anything weird about the eviction?"

Tony sighed, sitting back in his chair. "The whole thing was weird. Typically Buddy would be late on his rent. I'd charge him a late fee. Then I'd call him and threaten eviction. Then right before the end of the month he'd pay up, and sometimes even pay the following month. It never got to the courthouse. Never."

I frowned. "Why do you think he paid late?" Jake and Lottie had both said Buddy had been having financial troubles, but I wanted to hear what Tony had to say.

The developer held up his hands. "Heck if I know. At first I thought he was prioritizing other stuff. If Buddy had a chance to invest in something, or buy a used piece of equipment, he'd spend his money there and be short on rent. The last few months he always seemed to have plenty of money, though. I think by then he was just messing with me. When he skipped out, he owed three months back rent. I figured he'd been planning on moving out anyway and decided to stiff me what he owed. At least Buddy left the place in good condition, so I didn't have to spend thousands fixing holes in drywall or replacing the carpet. I kept his security deposit, but I was still out two months' rent, plus all the filing fees, plus what it cost to have his stuff hauled out of the farmhouse and to the dump."

"What was left in the house?" Lottie asked.

Tony shrugged. "Not much, to be honest. Some old furniture that wasn't worth squat. A few cartons of leftovers and some beer in the fridge. Toiletries, a couple of towels, plus a few clothes. CDs and about a dozen books. Some notepads and pencils."

Lottie and I exchanged a glance. "Did he leave any of the farming equipment behind?"

"Nope. His tractor and attachments weren't there and neither were any of his tools. When Deputy Cork met me to change the locks and clear everything out, Buddy was gone and so was his truck. The deputy went through the house, gave me the all clear, and I had my crew put everything out on the curb. We came back the next day and hauled whatever wasn't picked through to the dump." Tony looked down at his coffee as he said this, making me wonder about the truth to his statements.

"You didn't keep anything?" I watched Tony carefully. "I wouldn't blame you if you did. The guy skipped out owing you a bunch of money. If you wanted to grab a CD or two from what he'd abandoned, then it was kinda your right to do so."

Tony sighed and ran a hand through his wavy silver hair. "Trust me, I didn't want any of Buddy's music. I'm a country music kinda guy. I'm not going to pocket the dude's Metallica CDs."

I laughed. Not that I hadn't listened to the occasional Metallica back in the day, but I didn't have any of their CDs. Actually I didn't have CDs any more. They'd been sold off at yard sales ages ago. Nowadays everything I listened to was streamed.

"But…" Tony fiddled with his coffee cup. "Okay. Buddy left about twenty bales of nice hay in the barn. Probably wasn't right of me, but it was decent first-cut hay. It helped make up for what Buddy stiffed me."

"What the heck was Buddy doing?" Lottie wondered. "He moves most of his belongings out. Moves or sells his farm equipment and tools. It seems like he *was* going to stiff you on the rent and move on, but why didn't he sell the hay before he took off? People complained that he hadn't made his deliveries. He could have stayed an extra couple of weeks, sold that hay, and still have been gone before you and Sean showed up to kick him out."

"Maybe he didn't get a chance to sell the hay," I thought out loud.

"Buddy was a guy who liked everything to fall into place," Lottie commented. "He'd short bales, overcharge and underpay—and pay late whenever he could. But at the end of the day, he profited. Things always worked out for Buddy Hooper."

"Yeah." I thought of the body in the woods, trying to decide if I believed it was Buddy's or not. "Things worked out for Buddy Hooper. Until they didn't."

CHAPTER 9

*S*ierra arrived with our food and conversation turned to more mundane matters. Tony discussed the strip mall he was building as well as the other development they'd just begun to break ground on. I talked about the campground. Lottie went over Amanda's wedding plans. When we'd finished, Tony insisted on paying. Lottie asked him to call her if he thought of anything further in regards to Buddy's disappearance, then Tony walked us to her BMW, taking the opportunity to hug Lottie again before heading off to his own vehicle.

Once we were on the road, I turned to my friend.

"So…Tony." I wiggled my eyebrows. "I think that man has a thing for you 'Lottie-pop.'"

Lottie went red. "I'm married. Tony didn't pay any attention to me until I'd safely walked down the aisle with Scotty. The man is a flirt, but he likes to keep his flirting to married women."

I frowned. "Adultery is his thing?"

"Heavens, no. Tony feels safe flirting with married women because he knows they won't take him seriously. He dated Brenda Snell in college and we all thought they'd get married, but they broke up after *fifteen years*. Far as I know he's been single and a flirt ever since. Actually, he's always been a flirt, single or not."

"Fifteen years?" I choked a bit. "That's a long time to date someone without a ring on your finger."

Lottie nodded. "I know. After ten years, everyone just assumed Brenda was okay with that, but evidently not. Rumor has it she was the one who left."

"I can't say I blame her," I retorted.

"Me too." Lottie blew out a breath. "I shouldn't encourage Tony. He's such a flirt. But it's harmless, right?"

"Harmless," I agreed. "It's nice to have someone find you attractive. That doesn't seem to happen much once we cross the fifty-year mark. A good-looking man wants to compliment you and lament that you're married? Enjoy it, then go home to Scotty."

Her face fell a little, and for a second I wondered what I'd said wrong. Then I thought about my suspicions that things weren't ideal between Lottie and her husband.

"Amanda would say he's a total silver fox," Lottie said, her expression lightening.

"And I would agree."

It took us all of five minutes to drive to the outskirts of Reckless and into the self-storage parking lot. There was a small office building on our side of the tall, wire-topped fence that surrounded the rows of storage units. A gate blocked the entrance, a security keypad on a metal pole to the side of the gate. Lottie and I got out of her BMW and headed into the office where a tall, gaunt, elderly man sat behind a desk, playing some game on a Nintendo Switch.

"Hey Ernest. How's it going?" Lottie asked.

The man didn't even raise his eyes from the game. "Got

some blight going through my tomatoes, but the beans are doing good."

I turned to Lottie with raised eyebrows. "Game," she whispered, letting me know that the tomatoes and beans he'd referred to weren't real.

"That's nice. Glad your beans are doing well," Lottie replied to the man. "Wondered if you'd have a few moments to answer some questions about a storage unit. Or maybe you could call Collette, if you're too busy growing beans and fighting off tomato blight."

The mention of Collette got the man moving. He hit a button on the Nintendo and set it aside. "No need to involve my wife, Lottie. You needing a storage unit? Ten-by-ten, or one of the larger ones? Climate control, or outside?"

"Actually we want to ask you about any unit rentals by Buddy Hooper in the last year," I spoke up.

Ernest scowled. "I'm not happy with Buddy Hooper. He paid for three months up front, then we got nothing. After five months, we repo'd his unit and auctioned off the contents."

Lottie practically bounced with excitement. "When did he rent the unit? And when did he stop paying?"

Ernest pulled a keyboard over in front of him and began typing. "Came in the first of May and rented one of our larger units. Paid through July. We never got anything after that. Started sending him notices by mail and e-mail in August. Even called his phone. We never heard anything from him, so per our contract terms, we took possession and auctioned it off this past January."

"Any idea what was in the unit?" I asked him.

I had no idea how these storage unit auctions went. Did the business open the unit and inventory it prior to the auction? Did they sell it off sight-unseen? Did someone from the storage unit company stick around to see what was actually in the unit they'd just auctioned off, or grab their money and go?"

"Lot of boxes. Some furniture. A gaming computer, of all things." Ernest shook his head. "It was a nice computer, too. High-end stuff. You could totally run some virtual reality games off of that thing. That plus the laptop and the cell phones were worth a whole lot more than what was owed on the unit. Can't believe Buddy would have just let all that go when he could have sold it and made some good money."

"He had a gaming computer, a laptop, and several cell phones in his storage unit?" I frowned, wondering if Buddy had been into video games. It didn't fit with the picture I had of the guy, but people defied stereotypes all the time. A hay farmer could absolutely want to play computer games in his spare time and want the latest in cell phone technology.

Ernest nodded. "They were all in the box too. Guy never even used them, never even opened the boxes. Those cell phones were models that had just been released the month he'd rented the storage unit too."

New, in-the-box electronics. A barn full of good hay. I didn't think Buddy was the kind of guy to leave all that behind. All of this pointed to some sort of foul play in the man's disappearance.

"What address did Buddy give for billing?" Lottie asked.

Ernest typed, then gave us the address for Tony's farmhouse—the one Buddy had been evicted from in July.

"And the phone number?" Lottie wrote down both bits of information, then turned to me with her eyebrows raised.

"Who bought the unit when you auctioned it off?" I asked Ernest.

"Ellen Preston," he said.

* * *

"It makes sense," Lottie pointed out as we drove to Ellen Preston's house. "She runs one of those online stores for stuff she picks up at yard sales and auctions. It must be profitable because she quit her job a couple of years back and started doing this full-time."

"There aren't two Ellen Prestons in Reckless are there? Because it's kinda weird that a woman who was there at the tracking event where Elvis found the body is the same one who bought the contents of Buddy Hooper's storage unit."

"There's only one Ellen Preston. Reckless isn't a big town," Lottie explained. "There's going to be all sorts of coincidences like this. And like I said, she's got a reason to be buying the stuff from his storage unit. She probably buys a bunch of abandoned storage units for her business, and some of those units might have been owned by friends of neighbors, or the clerk at the convenience store she gets her gas from."

"Basically everyone in Reckless has six degrees of separation from everyone else," I said.

Lottie laughed. "More like four degrees of separation."

We pulled into the driveway of a small, brick, ranch-style home. Huge hydrangeas with snowball-white blooms flanked the porch, and pink impatiens filled the window boxes. The garage was missing the typical roll-up door. A vinyl-sided section was in its place with a window to the right and a door to the left. The sign over the door said "Found Treasures" in letters stylized to look like they were cut from a magazine. I could hear music coming from the garage as well as a noise that sounded like someone taping up a box.

Lottie knocked then opened the door a crack to peek in "Helloooo? Ellen?"

The volume on the music lowered. "Hey Lottie! Come on in. Are you looking for something in particular? I just got in a bunch of these old typewriters. Planning to make jewelry out of the ones that are too broken to fix."

"Ooo, that sounds like fun." Lottie swung the door open and we walked in.

Harper, Ellen's yellow Lab that I'd met at the tracking event, hopped up from a pillow and walked over to greet us. I scratched the dog's head and looked around, marveling at how neat and organized the business was. A desk sat against the back wall with a laptop, a printer and an additional monitor. Long tables took up one entire wall. On them were boxes, a scale, and separate piles of goods with what I assumed was a packing slip or invoice on top. Above one table hung a giant roll of bubble wrap. The rest of the garage was filled with shelves, all of them labeled and loaded with boxes and a variety of items. There were lamps, fancy clocks, pottery, and crystal decanters. One shelf held a large number of porcelain figurines, and the other was filled with an assortment of typewriters that looked like something my mother would have used back in the '70s.

"Sassy!" Ellen's voice interrupted my perusal of her wares. "It's good to see you again. I hope what happened at the tracking event didn't scare you off from the Reckless Sniffers Club."

"Elvis's poor performance might have scared me off from the club," I said with a smile. "We clearly need more remedial work before hitting the field again."

"Hey, he found that body. It might not be what you sent him after, but that was still a good result in my opinion. Maybe Elvis is better suited as a cadaver dog, or in search and rescue."

"He *is* better at search and rescue than scent detection." I motioned toward Lottie. "Actually we didn't come to buy something or talk tracking. We heard from Ernest over at the self-storage place that you bought a unit at auction in January that had belonged to Buddy Hooper."

"I did. Sometimes the contents of those units hold some real treasures." She shrugged. "And sometimes they're total duds. One unit I bought this year had moldy paintings, a stained twin-sized mattress, and a box of eight-track tapes. I had to haul most of it to the dump. Thankfully the eight-track tapes sold so I ended up breaking even on the deal."

Her tone was light and casual, but I'd seen her stiffen when I'd mentioned Buddy's name. Had there been a particular reason she'd bought the contents of his storage unit instead of another? Or maybe there had been something inside the unit she didn't want to discuss.

"I heard he had a bunch of brand-new electronic equipment in there," Lottie chimed in. "Who keeps new in-the-box cell phones in a storage unit? Wouldn't he be using them? And why would he have purchased more than one? And Ernest said there was a really nice gaming computer and a laptop in there as well—all of them new and in-the-box."

Ellen nodded. "Mike Allen bought the electronics off me the same day. He was there to bid on the storage unit, but once the price got up a bit, he dropped off. I don't blame him. I was taking a huge risk paying what I did for that unit without knowing what was inside."

"Mike Allen?" I exchanged a confused glance with Lottie. "Isn't he a VP at Rio Grande Electronics? Why would he want cell phones and computers from a storage unit when he could probably get them for cost from where he works?"

Ellen shrugged. "Heck if I know. I assumed he had enough of that stuff at home already, but when he offered to buy the gaming computer, the laptop, and the cell phones, I wasn't going to ask questions. Mike offered me two grand cash when he saw what was in the unit after I'd bought it and opened the door. I don't sell electronics through my store, and didn't need any of that stuff, so I was happy to take the money. It was the quickest sale on a storage unit I'd ever made. Two grand ten minutes after winning the bid? I'll take that any day."

Clearly I was in the wrong business. Ellen probably didn't pay more than three or four hundred at auction for storage units, and the electronics in Buddy's alone had made her two thousand dollars. Although, that was probably a crazy streak of luck. As she'd said, most of the storage units she bought probably didn't have anything but junk.

"What else was in the storage unit?" I asked her.

"Some furniture. Dishes, pots and pans, and housewares. Things like a blender, an Instant Pot, a television, winter coats. Boxes of paperwork. Boxes of clothes. Normal things that people store in a self-storage unit."

When they're in between houses, maybe. Unless Buddy was moving in with someone else for a while, he'd want his dishes and television. And he would have wanted to claim the rest of it. None of that was junk, it was all the kind of stuff that would cost a lot of money to replace, that people took with them from one place to another.

"Wow, you must have made bank on all that," Lottie commented.

Ellen flinched. "Yeah."

The one word was flat, full of...grief? Had there had been personal reasons Ellen had bought the contents of Buddy's storage unit?

"You didn't sell it," I said with all the sympathy I could muster. "You couldn't sell it. Besides the electronics, you kept everything, didn't you?"

Ellen's lips trembled. She clamped them tight, then nodded.

Lottie's eyes widened. She shot me a quick look before

turning to Ellen. "I heard you all had been dating, but I thought that was just gossip."

What? Ellen and Buddy Hooper? The industrious eBay entrepreneur and the farmer who skimmed on his deliveries, shorted people, and generally weaseled everyone he did business with? Ellen and *Buddy?*

She flushed. "We dated a couple of years ago. Buddy broke things off after a few months. He told me he had some opportunity that was going to take him out of the area, but then I heard he was seeing Joy Ann over at the Chat-n-Chew. So I got dumped. And stupid me, I bid way too much on his storage unit when it came up for auction. And I kept everything except for what Mike Allen bought off of me that day."

Ellen clearly had feelings for the guy that hadn't been returned. He'd lied to her about his plans to leave town, then had taken up with someone else. She wouldn't be the first jilted lover to murder her ex. Admittedly, Ellen didn't seem like the type, but I really didn't know her beyond that one day at the tracking event.

"Oh Ellen." Lottie made a "tsk" noise. "You're too good to be slumming it with Buddy Hooper. He's not a bad looking guy, but he's...*Buddy Hooper.*"

Ellen glared at her. "You see anyone else asking me out? No? Well, me neither. I spent a year on one of those dating apps and they couldn't match me with anyone closer than an hour's drive away. There's not a lot of eligible guys in Reckless. And Buddy treated me good. It was nice having some companionship for once. And...and it was really nice having *companionship*, if you know what I mean."

I felt for Ellen, really I did. I'd done the rounds of dating after I'd felt I'd recovered sufficiently from my divorce, but nothing had ever come of those casual dates and eventually I'd just given up, deciding to be happy as a single woman. I had no idea what Ellen's past was, but dating in her forties had to be difficult, especially in a small town where everyone knew each other.

Buddy had broken things off with some lame excuse and started going out with Joy Ann over at the Chat-n-Chew. But *was* it a lame excuse? Maybe premature, but Buddy clearly did intend to leave the area. He'd let his lease go into eviction. He'd moved the majority of his belongings into a storage unit. I wondered what he'd told Joy Ann about his intentions, because she hadn't reported him missing right after he'd vanished.

An opportunity that would take him out of the area. I wondered if there was any truth to that. And if so, what was the opportunity? Had Buddy expected to eventually return to Reckless, or did he plan on having a truck pick up his belongs from the storage unit and drive them to wherever he'd moved—wherever this "opportunity" was?

Lottie sighed. "I know there aren't a lot of single guys in Reckless. I shouldn't have said that, Ellen. If Buddy treated you well, and you were happy then...well, I'm sorry things didn't work out."

Ellen's eyes sparkled with tears and she blinked them away. "I did keep his stuff. I knew he had a storage unit and what number it was. The auctions for the units are listed in the papers, and I usually go, just to bid on one or two. When I saw Buddy's unit, I had to buy it."

Okay, she knew he had a storage unit and the number? "Did he have the storage unit when he was dating you?" I asked. "Did he maybe take you out there where he was dropping stuff off or picking stuff up?"

She flushed red again. "No. I probably sound like some psycho stalker, but I kept hoping he'd come back to me. I mean, Joy Ann? Good grief. What's she got that I don't have? Anyway, I sort of followed him around. From a distance. Real discreet-like so he didn't know. When I saw him bringing stuff to Reckless Self-Storage, I had a chat with Ernest and he told me the unit number that Buddy had rented."

I liked Ellen and felt sorry for her, but she was looking more and more like the murderer.

"You know that people are saying the body Elvis found in the woods is Buddy's," Lottie said, her voice kind.

Tears glistened in Ellen's eyes once more. "I...I don't want to believe that. But honestly, when I bought the storage unit and Ernest cut the lock off and opened the door, I feared the worst. I could see Buddy leaving the other stuff behind if he'd struck it rich somewhere, but all those electronics? He would have sold them. He was too obsessed with making money to leave something worth that much behind to be auctioned off."

"What do you think happened to him, Ellen?" I asked.

She shrugged, then wiped a hand across her eyes. "I don't know. Maybe he was planning to ditch the Marconi farm and rent, or buy, something else and something happened to him. Maybe he did have some big deal going on that would take him out of town, and that deal was the end of him. I don't know if that body your dog found was Buddy, but I think he's dead. He always had some scam going, something just over the line of what was legal. It was never enough to get him in trouble with the law, but maybe it was enough to get him killed."

I flinched at the raw emotion in her voice.

"Maybe I should have kept an eye on him," Ellen said. "I know I was borderline stalking, but if I'd kept following him, if I'd watched him more then maybe he'd still be alive. At least I could have reported to the police when he went missing and maybe got them to investigate early enough to actually have some leads. But I started to feel like an idiot, like someone who was obsessing over a man who'd dumped her. So I let him be. And seven months later I was buying the stuff in his storage unit."

I exchanged a glance with Lottie, not sure how to proceed with this whole thing. Ellen had clearly loved Buddy. I didn't think that had crossed into the kind of obsession that would lead her to kill him, but either way, Ellen might have information that might shed some light on what happened to Buddy—even if the body in the woods hadn't been his.

Wasn't it always the spouse? The jilted lover? I hated to think that Ellen might have killed Buddy, but the logical part of my brain wasn't willing to rule out the possibility.

"You still have the stuff from the storage unit?" Lottie asked.

Ellen nodded. "It's in my house. I couldn't sell it, so I took it in there. I haven't even worked up the nerve to go through most of the boxes."

"Can we see it?" I asked, worried that she'd be protective over Buddy's belongings. "Maybe there's something there that could help us figure out what happened to him."

That seemed to appeal to Ellen. She agreed to let us go through Buddy's stuff and showed us in through the ranch house to a back bedroom where an entire garage sale worth of items was taking up half the room.

Leaving us there, Ellen and Harper went back to package up their shipments for the day. Lottie and I surveyed the task at hand, then got to it, sorting through kitchen appliances, household goods, and boxes that held towels, clothes, and an assortment of knickknacks, pictures, and books.

"When do you have to be back at the campground?" Lottie asked.

I looked at my watch. "I'm okay hanging here another hour, but then I really should get back. I don't want to leave Mom and Austin to handle everything solo too long. And

Austin leaves at five. I especially don't want Mom to have to run things by herself."

"Then we better hustle," Lottie said, diving into the first bunch of boxes.

We quickly ruled out the ones that held personal belongings, and ended up with four large boxes with papers that the pair of us felt needed more scrutiny than we could give here today. We pushed those heavy boxes aside, then went out to ask Ellen if we could possibly take them home to go over their contents later. She was initially reluctant to let anything of Buddy's out of her house, but Lottie eventually convinced her that having us look through them was better than just having them sit in a back bedroom for years until she felt strong enough to do it herself.

Lottie and I both got our strength training in for the day hauling those boxes out and putting them into the trunk of her BMW sedan. The brief glimpse we'd taken had shown that the weighty boxes held things like receipts, bank statements, tax returns, and other paperwork. I anticipated a boring few evenings going through the contents, but if anything would give us a hint at where Buddy had ended up, this paperwork might. Crime shows were full of dramatic reveals and chases through dark alleys, but I got the feeling that real-life crimes were mostly solved through a meticulous perusal of paperwork and boring dogged detective work. It might not be thrilling, but I was up to the task.

Once we were back at the campground, I instructed Lottie to pull around to the house. After parking, we flipped coins to determine who got which of the boxes, then Lottie helped me carry my two inside. I waved her off, then headed over to the camp store to relieve Mom.

Mom was relaxing behind the counter, reading a book. Elvis was at her side, snoozing on his pillow. The hound looked up at me, then promptly went back to sleep. Mom greeted me, then went back to reading her book.

I felt a wave of relief. Guilt had always hung over me like a black cloud when I left Mom alone at the campground. She was supposed to be retired and enjoying life, not sitting behind the register in my campground's store while I ran around with my friend and solved mysteries. Mom had repeatedly told me she enjoyed helping out and feeling productive, and that I should be able to take time off for myself, but I still felt guilty.

But seeing her relaxed and chill, with my dog equally relaxed and chill by her side...it alleviated the guilt. This wasn't a chore for her. And I *did* need my time off so I could be energetic and recharged during the long hours I spent managing the campground.

"Any new news on the mystery?" Mom said, sticking her bookmark in the book and setting it aside.

I told her about the meeting with Tony, the discoveries at the storage place, and what we'd learned from Ellen Preston.

"Think there's anything in those boxes?" Mom asked.

I shrugged. "We'll see. But I'm more convinced than ever that something happened to Buddy Perkins. Who leaves behind a bunch of sellable hay? And more to the point, who abandons a storage unit full of not only personal items, but valuable electronics that could have been easily sold or even pawned."

"Couldn't have been pawned if they were stolen," Mom said, startling me with the observation. "Pawnshops have to report details of their purchases or collateral for pawns to the police. They go through stolen goods reports, and if they match, they can seize the items. Pawnshops need to hold everything for about a week until they can be released for sale, just in case something was brought in from a crime."

I blinked at her. "But he still could have sold it all

privately. The stuff was in boxes and clearly brand-new. And as sketchy as Buddy Hooper was, I can't see him as the type to shoplift electronics from a store."

"There's plenty of stolen goods going around," Mom pointed out. "I had friends who openly bragged about getting their living room furniture 'out of the back of some truck.' Someone would divert a shipment, sell it in a back alley, then muddy up the paperwork so the company would have no idea where the heck the stuff had gone, or if it had even been received at all."

"But what would the profit margin be?" I asked. "If Buddy had bought some stolen electronics off the back of a truck, then tried to sell it privately, I can't see that the money would be worth the effort. He'd make more selling bales of hay." I frowned. "But Mike Allen did pay Ellen Preston two grand for the electronics, so maybe I'm wrong."

"He's the big-wig executive that works for Rio Grande and is president of the tracking club?" Mom waited for my nod. "I wonder why he'd bother buying all that from a storage unit? Or why he was even there bidding on a storage unit at all. I mean, two grand? The cell phones and laptop were probably about eighteen-hundred in retail, and the gaming computer another twelve hundred in retail. That's three grand retail, and probably only about a thousand wholesale or black-market. If he'd been some dude-off-the-street who'd offered Ellen six hundred for the lot, then I'd understand. But an executive who could probably get all of that for cost? Why did he pay that? Why was he even there?"

Mom was right, and I didn't have any answers to her questions. Why was Mike there? And why buy the electronics from Buddy's storage unit when he could surely get them cheaper from his job?

CHAPTER 10

uesday I was up early as usual to walk Elvis and get the coffee brewing at the camp store. After Flora had come and gone with the day's deliveries, I took my mug of coffee out onto the porch and watched the sunrise. The orange-streaked gray was just starting to turn blue and gold when Elvis jumped to his feet, tail wagging. With a deep chuffing noise he danced happily, looking down the drive. A second later I heard the sound of a vehicle on the gravel, and Jake's truck appeared towing his boat and trailer.

I waved, expecting him to drive on down to the ramp and was surprise when he parked in the lot and walked toward the store.

"I left my thermos of coffee on the kitchen counter," he said as he climbed the stairs. "Figured it would be easier to just buy some than find a place to turn around with my trailer to get mine."

Jake lived across the road and up the mountain. Technically he was my neighbor, but he wasn't exactly walking distance. And I was pretty sure he would have had to go all the way down to the road to find a turnaround spot.

He stopped to pet Elvis and I stood.

"Do want to borrow a thermos?" I wasn't sure how much coffee Jake intended on drinking while fishing, and my largest cup only held twenty ounces.

"If it's not any trouble. Or I could buy one. There's no harm in having a spare."

"We don't sell them, but I've got one in the house you can borrow." I motioned for him to sit. "You hang out and keep Elvis company and let any customers know I'll be right back."

Before he could protest I was off the porch and jogging to the house.

My thermos was the matte green Stanley one that my dad had used since I was a child. He'd taken coffee to work in it. He'd used it when we were on long family road trips. It got packed along with the picnic basket and our camping gear. It had only ever held coffee and aside from a few cosmetic scratches, the thing was as good as new. I gave it a quick rinse with some hot water, then jogged back to the camp store.

Jake's eyes widened. "Whoa! I haven't seen one of those in ages. My Dad used to put his coffee in it every morning when he headed off to the job site. It would still be blisteringly hot ten hours later."

"This one was my dad's," I told him. "Which is why you have to promise to return it."

"Absolutely." He stood and followed me into the store.

"Are you a Breakfast Blend kind of guy, or a Dark Roast kind of guy," I asked. "Or Decaf."

He winced at the last one. "I better stick with Breakfast Blend. Gotta watch the caffeine now."

I unscrewed the cup and the cap and began to fill the thermos. "Oh, I know. If I have coffee after dinner, I'm up all night. If I keep it to a cup in the morning and maybe one in the afternoon, I'm fine, but more than that and I get the jitters."

"When I was a cop I used to drink three pots of the stuff a day. Now I'm down to one pot a day," he said with a laugh.

I stopped the coffee flow, peeked in the thermos to make sure I'd filled it up enough, then screwed the lid on. "You know, I meant it when I said you should just leave your boat here. It seems silly for you to be driving it back and forth almost every day when I've got these slips sitting empty."

"You'll need those slips for you own boats," he countered.

"I've got two boats, neither of which work right now, and four slips." I reminded him as I handed him the thermos. "None of my guests have used them so far. They seem happy with the canoes and kayaks. And it's not like I have guests coming in by water or anything. We're friends, Jake. You like to fish. I've got four slips I'm not using. It'll save you from having to launch your boat each time."

"Okay. But I'll find a way to repay the favor. And if you ever need all four of your slips, let me know. Oh." He dug in his pocket and handed me a piece of paper. "There's another reason I came into the store. I heard over at Bait and Beer that Andy Treeling has some motors for sale. Sounds like they might be the right size for your pontoon boat. Here's his number if you'd like to give him a call."

"Thanks." I put the paper in my pocket. "I really don't know anything about boats or motors. Do you think if I write down the make and model of the pontoon boat, Andy will know if the motor will work?"

"He might." Jake hesitated. "I can go with you if you like. I don't claim to be a boat expert or anything, but I can make sure the motor is the right size, that it's in good repair and that you get a good deal. Andy's not the kind of guy who'd rip someone off, but it doesn't hurt to know the going rate."

"I'd really appreciate that." I smiled, feeling better about potentially spending hundreds of dollars on a motor with Jake weighing in on the purchase.

"It's the least I could do with you letting me use your boat launch and now your slip." He held up the thermos. "I'll be back in around lunchtime. Just text me and let me know when you're meeting Andy and I'll swing by to pick you up. I figure if you buy the motor, we can haul it back easier in the bed of my truck."

"Will do." I watched him leave, thinking that we'd probably be going over this evening. I was off as soon as Mom got in around ten, but I remembered Andy telling me he worked in finance at some company I'd never heard of over in Derwood. He probably didn't even get home until after five.

Which would leave me the whole day to hike, or canoe, or relax on the sandy beach by the lake with a book. Or go through those boxes of Buddy Hooper's papers that Lottie and I had brought back from Ellen's. I was pretty sure Lottie had already gone through her boxes, and I didn't want to seem like a slacker in comparison.

It was supposed to be hot today, so maybe I'd take Elvis for a hike, then after lunch I'd hang out in the air-conditioned house and go through the papers. I was deciding which activity appealed the most when another vehicle pulled down the drive to park in front of the camp store. Tony Marconi got out of the white SUV, then grabbed a canvas bag from the backseat and slung it across his shoulder before heading up the porch steps.

I met him out front, Elvis by my side. "Morning, Tony! I'm guessing you're here to check out the beach?"

"If it's not too much trouble." He winced. "I know it's early. Sorry about coming by at such an uncivilized hour of the morning. I'm always up at five, and I forget that not everyone else is an early bird."

"I'm an early bird myself. Gotta get that worm," I joked. "Let me flip the sign on the store and we'll walk on down."

Elvis walked along with us. Tony and I waved at Jake as his fishing boat went by, then the developer got to work, shoving a ruler down into the sand, taking notes, and even rolling up his pants and taking his shoes off to wade into the water.

I felt silly standing around watching him. There wasn't anything I could contribute knowledge-wise to any of this. The beach had been put in long before I'd bought the camp-ground, and I didn't know anything about the engineering around how it was built. It wasn't like I needed to watch Tony. He wasn't likely to harass the two guests sitting over by the dock drinking their coffee. There was nothing to steal besides some faded umbrellas. Not that I expected Tony to steal anything.

Most of the guests who'd needed something from the camp store had already been by. I didn't have anything else to do, so I stood around, feeling silly as I watched the man measure and mutter to himself.

"How are things going with the historian-diver?" I asked as Tony made more notes. "Did they find anything down there? Are you free to start putting in the fill dirt and the sand?"

"They're coming out late Wednesday afternoon." Tony rolled his eyes. "I've never seen people so excited about poking around in the bottom of a muddy lake before. The woman on the phone practically talked my ear off about history, and how old maps hinted that there might have been a church somewhere near where I'm putting in the beach. I hope they don't find it, or things will be held up for months while they gleefully swim around taking pictures and hauling rotted stuff up from the lake."

"Are these people from the state historical commission, or the local Savage Lake Historical Society?" I asked him.

"The local group. The state contracted them to do the dive so instead of one guy with a metal detector, I'm getting five enthusiasts with all kinds of equipment and underwater cameras."

I secretly hoped they found something. Not that I wanted Tony's development delayed. He obviously had a lot of money tied up in this project, and needed to get the beach in and those other houses sold. But a church! I wondered how well preserved it would be after roughly a hundred years under water.

I made some sympathetic comment and watched as Tony finished his notes. After he'd put everything back into his canvas bag, I walked him back to his car, noting that the white SUV looked like he'd just washed it. I wondered if he had to run it through the car wash every evening to get the dirt from the construction site off of it, or if he'd washed it over the weekend.

"You know, when we were in high school, I had the biggest crush on Lottie," Tony told me with a lopsided smile.

"Really?" I wasn't sure how to respond to that. His comment seemed to come out of nowhere, and in spite of Lottie's assurances that he was a harmless flirt, I didn't quite trust Tony's motives when it came to my friend. His confession of a childhood crush made me even more uncomfortable. Did he expect me to pass this information on to Lottie? To play the matchmaker between him and my married friend?

"Yes, really." He put his canvas bag in the backseat, then turned to face me. "I was the class clown, skinny with braces and acne. She was a majorette, leader of the debate club, head of the yearbook committee, and homecoming queen our junior year. I used to go to football games just to watch her at halftime marching around the field, twirling her baton."

I couldn't help but smile, intrigued by this glimpse into my friend's past.

"I never told her how I felt," Tony continued. "For all my pranks and jokes I was really shy back then. I still kind of am. Flirting is fun when it's clearly not going to go anywhere. If I'm actually interested in a woman I turn into a stammering idiot."

"Oh, I find that hard to believe." I forced a laugh, unable to imagine smooth-talking Tony as a stammering idiot.

"Seriously. Somehow I managed to actually start dating after high school." He shook his head. "Lottie and I went to separate colleges and on to separate lives. She married Scotty, and had kids. I never married, although I did once have a long relationship, and never had kids."

"Not everyone wants to get married or have kids." I hesitated, trying to think of something to say that would make it clear I wasn't going to support any current romantic ideas he might have about my *married* friend.

"That's me." He shrugged. "Honestly, I never really wanted children and although I like having the companionship of a girlfriend, I'm not sure I ever really wanted marriage either. I'm happy with the way things are. I know that sounds weird in a society where marriage and kids are expected and people who are single for life are looked at with pity, but I'm truly happy."

I suddenly wondered if I'd jumped to conclusions and Tony wasn't contemplating some seduction of my friend. Maybe he was just making conversation. Lottie was our only real connection, so he'd thought a story from their past, of his childhood crush would make good small talk? His comment about children and marriage felt honest, and he certainly hadn't been a stammering idiot when he'd met

Lottie and me for lunch, so perhaps his flirting was like Lottie had said—harmless with no real intent behind it.

"I'm happy being single as well," I said, feeling that maybe I should share a little myself. "My ex and I split up decades ago, and I never remarried. We had one child—our son Colton—but I never felt the need to have any more or to get married again."

Although my circumstances were different than Tony's. My husband had cheated on me and left me for his mistress, and I was pretty sure my bitterness over that had carried into my brief post-divorce dating life and my current outlook. It probably was the reason I suspected Tony of wanting to have an affair with Lottie.

Tony opened the driver's door and climbed in. "People think Lottie is silly, that she's nothing but a flighty gossip, an empty-nest homemaker with no smarts or skills. They're wrong. She's shrewd. And she's loyal. There's no better friend in the world than Lottie Sinclair."

I voiced my agreement, then watched as Tony navigated his car out of the parking lot and down the drive. The man had once been in love with Lottie, and I got the feeling that love had never gone away. Perhaps that had been the reason he'd not been able to commit to the long-term girlfriend.

It gave me a lot to think about. Even though I wasn't a huge fan of Scotty, I'd never really met the man. At the end of the day, Lottie loved him and that was all that mattered. Whatever was going on in their marriage, it wasn't my place to judge. And it certainly wasn't my place to imagine the sort of infidelity that had spelled the end of my own marriage and given me endless heartbreak in every opposite-sex interaction.

No, it wasn't my place at all to stick my nose into any of this.

CHAPTER 11

J texted Andy as soon as Tony had left, letting him know that I was interested in purchasing a used motor for the pontoon boat. He texted back right away, giving me his address and asking if I could meet him there around five-thirty tonight.

I agreed, then sent Jake a quick text with the information. If he couldn't make it tonight, I'd still go out to Andy's and take a look at what he had. I didn't have to make a decision today. If the motor looked good and the price was right, I could always ask Jake to go with me another time to see it, or ask Austin if Jake wasn't free.

Mom came in at ten. Elvis and I left her in charge of the camp store while I still went back and forth about what I'd like to do with the rest of my day. I'd been thinking about swinging by the house for my daypack, some water and snacks, and Elvis's own backpack to go on a hike, but as I exited the store I saw Austin's truck parked by the building we kept the boats in. Walking around the corner of the store, I noticed he wasn't alone. There was another boy with him, a red bandana covering his head. He wore jeans and a white tank that contrasted sharply with his ebony skin. Next to the boy stood a girl, tall and lean with tanned skin and her dark hair in braids. The three of them turned as we approached, and Elvis strained at the leash, wanting to greet our visitors.

"Is it okay if I let my dog off the leash?" I called out. "He's friendly."

"Sure. I love dogs," the boy announced.

The girl grinned. "Is that a bloodhound? What a hand-some boy. You're a good boy, aren't you? Such a good boy!"

I could barely get the leash unsnapped from Elvis's collar before he was off and running toward the kids, his tail high and wagging like crazy. The hound loved everyone, but he especially liked people who called him a "good boy."

Everyone made a big fuss over Elvis, then the hound found something interesting to sniff and suddenly the kids fell off his radar. I kept him in sight, ready to call back if he got too far, as Austin made the introductions.

"Guys, this is Miss Sassy. She owns the campground. Miss Sassy, this is Greg. He's in a vo-tech program at the community college for automotive bodywork and restoration. He spent a lot of time designing, making, and flying model aircraft with his dad, so he knows how to do fiberglass repairs."

"I'm not an expert," Greg said with an embarrassed smile. "And boats aren't the same as those planes Dad and I put together, but the basics of fiberglass repair are the same. Austin said your boat had a hole in it and asked me to take a look. I doubt I can fix it, but I can take some pictures and get you a quote from the marina."

"That's wonderful. Thank you." I'd decided to focus on the pontoon boat this year, but it would still be good to have a quote so I could either budget for the Baycraft repairs, or make the decision to scrap it.

"This is Savannah." Austin motioned toward the girl.

"She's a senior this year and completed two years of the small engine and automotive repair tech program our high school runs with the community college. This fall she's taking an eighteen-month program in diesel engine repair."

"I haven't decided if I'm going to specialize in large trucks, heavy equipment, or ships," Savannah said with a quick smile. "I haven't taken a look yet, but I'm pretty sure I can get your speedboat started."

That would be one less thing I'd need to worry about. And if I decided to scrap it, having a working engine might mean I'd get some decent money in salvage.

"I really appreciate this," I told them. "If you need a drink or a snack, stop in the camp store. My mother's in there now, but just let her know you both are working with Austin on the boats and to put anything on the owner's tab."

I might regret the snack offer. Teenagers were bottomless pits when it came to food. When Colton was in high school, he and his friends' raids on my pantry and fridge had nearly bankrupted me. But I was happy to have Austin's friends here helping out, so I wouldn't begrudge them a few bags of chips and sodas.

The three teens went into the barn to check out the Baycraft. I whistled for Elvis, snapped his leash back on when he ran back to me, then followed them in. Austin had cleaned the boat and it did look nice until we got around to the left side.

Was that starboard? Port? I'd probably need to start remembering these things.

"What do you think happened to it?" Austin asked as we all stared at the hole in the boat. "Did someone run it into some rocks, or maybe the dock?"

Greg lifted one shoulder. "I think it's more likely that someone ran it into something while it was on the trailer. Maybe they weren't too careful backing it in. See how there's a scrape here, and how the hole is kinda round? Rocks scrape, but I think there'd be a different shaped hole if this was from hitting some rocks. And these boats are sturdy. It would take more than just glancing off some rocks in shallow water to cause this. Plus if the boat was going fast and someone sideswiped a rock hard enough to punch through the hull, then there would be a long gash, and this boat would probably be at the bottom the lake, not parked here in your garage."

"Same with if they hit a dock," Savannah added. "I'd expect to see damage in the front if that happened. I agree with Greg. I think someone was backing it in to the garage, and hit something."

"Sucks," Austin said.

"Sucks," the other two agreed.

Yeah, it did.

I couldn't rule out that the previous owner, Len Trout, had damaged the boat and just had never gotten around to fixing it, but I was going to blame this on the former handyman. Daryl Butts had been a horrible handyman from what I'd seen. After Len had died, repairs hadn't been made even though he'd continued to draw a salary from the estate. I still suspected he'd stolen the motor off the pontoon boat. It wasn't a stretch to think he'd damaged the Baycraft and just never let Len or his sons know about it.

But all that was water under the bridge—or inside the boat unless I managed to get this thing fixed. I left the kids to work on the boats and went back to the house with Elvis, suddenly not interested in a hike. I needed something to take my mind off finances and the boats, and the air-conditioning in the house was especially appealing today.

. . .

I MADE myself a turkey and swiss on rye, put Elvis on the screened-in porch so my sandwich would be safe from any sneak-attack, then sat down to go through one of the boxes Lottie and I had brought back from Ellen's.

As I emptied it out, I realized paperwork wasn't the only thing in this box. Smack in the middle of it all was a box, still sealed and wrapped in plastic.

It was a GPS collar for a dog—the higher-end model that I'd passed over when I'd been looking to buy one for Elvis. I turned the box over and read the information on the back, then pulled my laptop over and typed the model number into the search bar.

Fifteen hundred dollars from Rio Grande Electronics, and slightly more at other retailers. And it had just been released in May of last year.

Why the heck did Buddy have this? Why was it unopened and buried in a box of personal papers? If someone spent that kind of money on a tracking collar, then why hadn't they opened it up and actually used it?

Did Buddy even have a dog? My heart suddenly lurched, worried about this possibly imagined canine. What had happened to the dog? Had it been left in the house, starving and dehydrated, until Tony finalized the eviction? I'm sure he would have mentioned at lunch that he'd found either an emaciated or a deceased dog when he and Deputy Sean Cook showed up to clear Buddy's belongings out. Had Buddy sold the dog? Taken it to the shelter? Had the murderer killed the dog as well as Buddy?

I was almost in tears at the thought. Was I a horrible person that the thought of Buddy's death didn't devastate me nearly as much as the thought that someone might have killed a dog that may not even have existed.

Andy said that Mike Allen had given the club members discounts on the GPS tracking collars that the dogs at the event were wearing. True, none of the collars the other dogs had been wearing this past Saturday were quite this high-end, but that didn't mean they weren't offered some kind of deal on any of the products Rio Grande sold. Maybe Buddy had bought this with a similar discount from Mike, hoping to resell it and make some money off of it rather than use it for his own dog. If Mike had been giving everyone a discount of half price, perhaps Buddy had thought he could sell it for ten or twenty percent off retail and make a little money.

And maybe that explained all the unopened electronics that Ellen had found in Buddy's storage unit. Did Mike make a habit of giving friends and neighbors steep discounts on products? Was Buddy using that friend discount to make some side money? That might be why Mike had been there to bid on the storage unit and why he'd offered Ellen cash for the computers and cell phones.

Turning the box over once more, I felt a twinge of envy. This was a really nice collar—much nicer than the one I'd ordered. Ellen had said she didn't really deal in this sort of resale item. Could I return the one I'd purchased, and maybe offer Ellen a few hundred dollars for this one instead? It felt a bit wrong to profit off of a dead man, but it seemed a terrible waste for this really nice GPS collar to just sit here in a box when someone, namely me, could put it to good use.

I reluctantly set the GPS collar aside, deciding I'd figure out whether to cross that ethical bridge or not another day, and turned to the other contents of the box.

The first thing I did was sort through the papers. There were a ton of unopened bank statements that I put in the first pile. I wasn't sure if Buddy just saved them all up until it was tax time, if he did his checkbook reconciling through online banking, or if he was just careless about his financial records, but he seemed to have saved every statement for the last three years.

The next stack was a pile of receipts, some printed and some hand-written. The third pile was credit card statements and other bills, and the last was miscellaneous stuff—catalogues and flyers that Buddy had thought worth keeping for some reason.

There was no correspondence in the box, but that didn't surprise me. No one wrote to each other anymore. Anything Buddy would have wanted to say to friends or family or a business associate probably would have been done over his phone via e-mail or text. I had no way of accessing those things, but if Stef confirmed the body Elvis found was Buddy's then I knew the police would be asking for those records.

I sat back and ate my sandwich as I surveyed the papers. When I finished my lunch, I let Elvis back in, grabbed a notepad and some paperclips from off the kitchen counter, and started with the miscellaneous pile first.

Most of the sales flyers were mailings from the co-op and other feed stores around the county. Buddy had circled the listings for the different types of hay and for straw and made some notes in the margins. I quickly realized that he was tracking the prices and most likely adjusting his own to stay competitive.

I clipped the flyers together, put them back in the box and made a note on my pad before pulling the pile of statements toward me.

Opening each of the envelopes, I put the statements in order of date, then paperclipped the envelopes together. I didn't think they'd be important, but I'd hate to throw something away only to find that the police really needed it later.

The sales flyers had been mildly interesting. The bank statements were mind-numbingly boring. Part of my issue was that I had no idea what I was looking for or how to categorize these transactions to get more of a bird's-eye look at the spending and deposits.

In the end I decided to look at deposits first. It was the most unenlightening thirty minutes of my life. Every deposit was cash with no way of tracing where the money had come from. That shouldn't have been a surprise. I'd assumed farmers would be writing checks for hay deliveries, but it seemed that Buddy ran a cash business. Perhaps he gave a discount or even required cash payment. I wouldn't fault the guy for that. Checks bounced, and I assumed lots of people might claim the check was in the mail when it, in fact, wasn't.

Scooting Elvis to one side of the couch, I got my laptop and started typing in each deposit and the date on a spreadsheet. When I was done going over the statements, I ran an overall average, an annual average, a monthly average, then plotted a line that forecasted future deposits based on the three years of history. It was something I'd done in my corporate job to calculate marketing and trade show spend and estimate budgets for coming years.

Pulling up the graph I sat back on the sofa and frowned. The prediction line was strong, but it was the monthly averages that really caught my attention. Buddy's business had been growing, but in the last year, it had shot up exponentially. Actually, in the last six months before he'd gone missing they'd gone up exponentially.

Buddy had vanished in June or July, and the deposits had increased significantly starting the prior December and through the spring deposits. It wasn't just the frequency that was driving the average up, it was one or two very large deposits each month that caused the spike in the chart. Did people really pay three thousand for a hay delivery? Or five thousand? Maybe that hadn't been one delivery, but twenty and Buddy just hadn't deposited the cash for a few weeks? But if Buddy could farm and sell *that* much hay, why had he

ELVIS FINDS A BONE

been in debt? What had changed in December that caused his business to suddenly turn a corner from slight-profit into runaway-success?

Why December? Did farmers need to purchase extra hay that year because of a hard winter? I pulled up the weather records for two years ago and compared it to the average, high, and low temps listed as well as the average snowfall and didn't see anything particularly alarming. There didn't seem to be any weather event that would indicate a run on hay deliveries. What if it wasn't excess demand that had driven the extra income, but an increase in prices? What if local hay prices had gone up due to a huge barn fire or a blight or something? Buddy followed prices very carefully and would have taken advantage of that.

I set the deposits aside and pulled the flyers out again, creating another tab on my spreadsheet to log the various hay prices for that three-year period. Then I ran the same predictive line, averages, and graphs. It didn't look like there was a huge uptick in prices the winter before Buddy had disappeared. Overlaying the two graphs brought that point home.

Buddy's income had grown significantly the six months before he'd vanished, and weather-driven hay demand or an increase in prices didn't explain that upsurge.

I made a quick note on the pad, wondering if Buddy had branched out into a second business. Hadn't Lottie mentioned he'd done hauling for people? Maybe that accounted for the extra money. If Buddy had managed to get a contract hauling for a business, that could be the reason for the extra, and if they paid him under the table, then it made sense that the deposits would be in cash.

I wrote down "hauling?" "income increase" and "large account balance" on my notepad, then pulled the statements back toward me to look at the daunting number of with-drawal transactions.

Buddy bought a lot with his debit card. Actually, the debit card activity and online payments were about ninety percent of the withdrawals, with checks few and far between. Once again, it was hard for me to get a bird's-eye view on the transactions with all the details on the stack of papers before me, so I pulled the laptop over, and began to enter every-thing, adding a column to categorize the expenditures as things like gas, equipment purchases, utilities, and dining. I wasn't halfway through the stack when my phone buzzed.

Back late from fishing. Going to shower and pick you up at five. Thanks again for letting me use the slip—and your thermos, Jake said.

I'll be ready, I replied.

I glanced at the clock and winced. It was my day off and I'd spent the majority of it going through stacks of papers and doing analysis on a spreadsheet. It wasn't how I'd envi-sioned my free time when I'd bought the campground, but this whole amateur sleuth thing wouldn't be all excitement and dramatic reveals. Sometimes crime solving involved a whole lot of drudgery.

But amateur was the key word in that whole scenario. And I only had forty minutes until Jake was to pick me up. So I sorted, rubber banded, and paperclipped the documents, putting sticky notes on each stack. Then I backed up my spreadsheet to the cloud, put my laptop away and went to get a shower of my own.

CHAPTER 12

Scrubbed and clean I surveyed the clothes in my closet with more than my usual care. I seriously wanted to put on one of the cute sundresses I'd bought on sale last summer, but I worried it might send the wrong message. Jake and I were friends, nothing more. He usually saw me in jeans or shorts, and my suddenly wearing a dress and strappy sandals might either give him ideas or send him running for the hills. In the end I opted for my usual shorts and T-shirt, but compromised by putting on some mascara and pink Chapstick in addition to my usual tinted moisturizer. I still eyed the strappy sandals, but decided my trusty sneakers would be the more practical choice.

Dressed and ready, I snapped the leash on Elvis and took him for a walk around the campground, waving and chatting with the guests that were back and prepping to make dinner. I arrived at the camp store ten minutes before Jake was to pick me up.

"How's it been today?" I asked Mom as Elvis and I entered the store.

"Slow." She waved her knitting needles at me and I saw a

circle of fuzzy blue attached to them. "I've made three hats for the hospital, did some Sudoku, and hacked into the military defense system." She laughed at my alarmed expression. "Just kidding! Well, just kidding about the hacking anyway. I did make three hats and play Sudoku."

I wouldn't put the hacking past my mother. She'd proven to be much more computer savvy than I'd ever thought, and I wouldn't put it past her to be nosing around less-than-secure government websites.

"Whew! I was worried that we were two minutes from being raided by a SWAT team with Black Hawk helicopters circling overhead." I walked behind the counter and hooked Elvis near his dog bed and water bowl. "Jake is picking me up soon to go look at that boat motor. Wish me luck."

"My fingers and toes are crossed." Mom held up her hands with her index and middle fingers crossed as proof. "I'm really looking forward to going out on the pontoon boat soon."

"Me too. If it's the right motor and the price is good, then we might be up and running this weekend," I promised. And if this one didn't work out, I'd continue to look for a used motor somewhere.

"Ooo, I almost forgot. This came for you." Mom scooted a box across the counter to me.

"It's Elvis's new GPS collar," I told her as I unboxed the item and removed it from the packaging. "We'll test it out tomorrow morning and see how well it works. I'm planning on using it when we go for hikes, at tracking events, and whenever Elvis is off leash."

Mom laughed. "That poor dog is going to have collars all the way up his neck."

I grimaced. "I know. Luckily he's got a long neck. And I'll probably use this in place of the e-collar since it has a vibration feature as well."

I glanced out the window and saw Jake's truck coming down the drive. Giving Elvis a quick head scratch, I said goodbye to Mom and headed out. He was just driving into the parking area, and pulled around in front of the porch when he saw me waiting on the steps. I climbed into the passenger side, shutting the door and putting on my seatbelt.

"Thanks again for this," I told him. "I know less than zero about boats and motors and really appreciate the help."

"It's no problem at all." He put the truck in gear when my seatbelt was buckled and we started down the drive.

Jake's truck was clean and neat—a good deal cleaner than mine was given that I tended to have Elvis in my passenger seat and bloodhounds covered everything in their vicinity with slobber. Add in the muddy paws, and my SUV always looked like I was coming back from a backcountry expedition. The sometimes deputy's truck was old and had been well used. There was a crack in the sun-faded dashboard, and an empty clip-on air freshener on the middle vent. The radio had been replaced with one that didn't quite fit in the dashboard space, and Jake had wedged what looked like a piece of wood into the gap. Under the dash was another set of electronics that I guessed was his police radio. Glancing behind me I saw a light bar mounted along the inside back of the cab. There wasn't one on the front dash, and I hadn't seen one on the roof when I'd climbed in, so I assumed Jake had one of those magnetic lights he could slap onto the roof from out of the driver's side window if needed.

The leather seats were worn smooth from use, and dirt had ground into the carpet, visible around the edges of the floor mats, that no vacuum could ever remove. The truck was old, and it wasn't fancy, but there wasn't a pile of fast-food bags or empty water bottles. And unlike *my* vehicle, his wasn't covered in dirt, fur, and dog slobber.

We sat in silence for a while, and although Jake seemed

perfectly content with the lack of conversation, I felt self-conscious and awkward. Should I ask him how his fishing went? Talk about the weather?

"I like the idea you had about doing history tours on the pontoon boat," Jake finally spoke up. "I think that might appeal to some of the people in the town as well. The ghost tour on the lake too. People know the general history of the area, but having a historian go into details would make the trip interesting. And people never tire of hearing ghost stories."

"Think it's something you might come out for?" I asked him. "I know you haven't been into the races, or the arts-and-crafts stuff, but maybe history on the lake has more of an appeal?"

He shot me a quick smile. "Will there be food? And beer?"

"I haven't decided yet. I'm thinking just some light finger food since actually serving meals on the pontoon boat would be a hassle. I was going to start with some sunset cruises and serve appetizers and champagne, then maybe expand food and drink offerings for the history and ghost tours if it makes sense logistically."

"I don't want to edge out any of your guests, but if you ever have an open spot, let me know," he told me.

I turned to face him, surprised. "For the sunset cruise as well? Or just the history and ghost tours?"

Jake didn't strike me as the champagne-and-finger-sandwiches kind of guy. Or the watching-a-sunset kind of guy either. But maybe I was wrong.

"It's not my go-to alcoholic beverage, but I won't turn up my nose at a glass of champagne. And I'd like to see the sunset from the lake. I'm always out in the mornings and back by mid-afternoon at the latest, so I've never seen a sunset from the water. Seen plenty of sunrises from my boat, but never a sunset."

"Well, we'll just have to remedy that situation." I was already thinking of a test voyage with Jake, Sierra, Lottie, Danielle, and Mom just to smooth out any wrinkles before I started selling the sunset cruises to our guests. It would be fun, and a good way to show appreciation to everyone for all they'd done to help me since I'd bought the campground.

We chatted about the upcoming town activities, the weather, and the new pizza place that was supposed to open later this month in the building that had once been home to a service station and quick-mart. We were hotly debating pizza toppings as we pulled into Andy's driveway. Jake, no surprise, was all about six different meat toppings, where I liked to reduce the protein and temper my sausage and pepperoni with onions, green peppers, mushrooms, and black olives.

"That's just wrong," Jake informed me as he put the truck in park. "Olives don't belong on a pizza."

"It's black olives. They're mild. Don't get me wrong, I love Kalamata olives and those green ones stuffed with garlic cloves, but I wouldn't force anyone to eat those on a pizza."

He rolled his eyes. "If you tell me you like anchovies on your pizza, you're walking home. And if you like pineapple, I'm going to have to arrest you. That's downright criminal."

"Anchovies on a Caesar salad? Totally. Load it up. On a pizza?" I wrinkled my nose. "I'd eat it if someone served it to me, but I don't think I'd order it."

"Thank God," he muttered under his breath.

"As for pineapple... I love grilled pineapple. And pineapple juice in a fruity umbrella drink. And dried pineapple in my trail mix. Not a fan of it on my pizza, though. I want savory toppings, not sweet ones when it comes to pizza."

Jake blew out a breath. "I seriously had my handcuffs ready to go for a moment there."

I blushed. I actually blushed like an eighteen-year-old girl because my mind went to a completely inappropriate area. To hide my reaction, I looked down, fumbled to unlatch my seatbelt, and opened the door.

"Glad I'm not going to spend the night in jail," I finally said when I'd corralled my thoughts a bit.

"Me too."

We walked up a zinnia-lined walkway to Andy's porch. His house was a square, two-story building. The only thing differentiating it from every other house on the block was the paint color, and the landscaping. It was a fairly new development, and I wondered if Tony Marconi's business had built these homes or not. Hopefully not. I liked to think that Tony had more imagination and that there was a variety of housing styles in his developments.

Jake pressed the doorbell and I heard Xanadu barking. The foxhound was by Andy's side when he opened the door, frantically trying to squeeze out past the man's leg and to freedom.

With some effort, Andy escaped through the doorway without letting Xanadu out.

"Sorry about that. She hasn't been for her walk yet, so she's a little hyper." Andy grimaced. "That's one of the things I hate about working all day. Xanadu's in a kennel until I can get home."

"But I'm sure she gets plenty of exercise before and after work," I said. "And on the weekends. You're probably doing scent work or tracking with her at least one day a week."

He nodded. "If there's not a Reckless Sniffers' event, then we're out working on our own. You should bring Elvis by some time when I take Xanadu out. She's used to hunting in a pack, and I'm sure she'd like the canine company."

"I'll definitely take you up on that, but I can't vouch for Elvis's ability to hunt with another dog. He's been tracking solo with me since I got him and I don't know much about his life before the rescue got him."

"Then we'll just have to see how he does."

I was here to see the boat motor, but since we were talking about tracking, it was the perfect opportunity to ask questions about what I'd found in that box this afternoon. "Hey, I wanted to ask about the GPS collars you all got last year. I went ahead and ordered one for Elvis, but I was wondering how much of a discount you all got from Mike?"

"Ten percent," Andy replied. "Not that I'm ungrateful for any savings, mind you, but it wasn't like we got them at cost or anything.

Ten percent. That certainly wouldn't be enough to buy and resell the electronics and make any sort of profit. But if Buddy wasn't selling all those new electronics, then what was he doing with them?

Andy turned to Jake. "Any news on that body Elvis found on Saturday? Everyone's saying it's Buddy Hooper."

I could swear that Jake rolled his eyes. "We haven't identified the body yet.

Andy turned back to me. "Buddy was a member of the Reckless Sniffers Club for a while there. Had a sweet liver-nosed red bloodhound named Daisy."

The dog! All my earlier worries came back. "What happened to Daisy? Did she vanish with Buddy? Did she die before he supposedly left?"

"He sold her to Dwight Patton a couple of years back," Andy said, much to my relief. "Dwight had been dying to buy her and finally offered Andy enough that he agreed to sell. Daisy is a good tracking dog, but her real skill is in finding downed deer and Dwight is an avid hunter."

I must have looked confused because Jake leaned forward to explain.

"Sometimes a hunter doesn't make a killing shot and the

deer runs. And sometimes no matter how hard you look, you can't track the injured deer down. One call and Buddy would come out with Daisy. She always found the deer."

"No hunter wants to let deer meat sit in the woods for critters to eat, and no hunter wants to leave a deer injured and in pain wandering around for days either," Andy added.

"Dwight treats that dog like royalty," Jake added, seeing the concern on my face. "Daisy goes everywhere with him."

I blew out a breath in relief. "I'm glad to hear that."

I was surprised at how enterprising Buddy Hooper was. Farming and selling hay. Hauling heavy equipment. Finding injured deer during hunting season. But why would he have purchased an expensive tracking collar *after* he'd sold his hound? He didn't have any use for the collar himself and with only a ten percent discount, he wouldn't have made much money buying then selling it.

"Anyway." Andy tossed a keychain in his hand. "You're here to see some boat motors, not hear me ramble on about hunting and dogs. They're all in the garage." He lifted a key fob, pressed a button, and the motorized garage door began to lift.

CHAPTER 13

*J*ake and I followed Andy, then stood outside the garage and waited until the door slowly made its way to the top. When it stopped, we all walked in.

Andy's garage clearly wasn't used for vehicular storage. There were three boat motors, two lawn tractors, and one of those zero-turn mowers.

"I refurbish and sell boat motors and lawn equipment," Andy said with a sheepish grin. "It's a little extra income."

"I can imagine," I said, wondering if everyone in Reckless had some sort of side-gig.

The motors looked huge. Maybe it was because they were up on stands with the part that usually was under the water exposed, but they still looked really big.

"I was reading some stuff online and it said I could use a ten horsepower motor," I commented, realizing that the numbers on the side of these motors were a lot larger than ten. Was that the horsepower? Or the model number? I honestly didn't know.

The expression on Jake and Andy's faces told me that my internet research had been way off base.

"Well, I don't have anything that small," Andy said. "I don't really want to tell you your business, Sassy, but even if I had a ten horsepower motor, I'd feel criminal selling it to you to use with that pontoon boat. Let me show you what I've got and how much I'm asking for them since you're here. If you want to think about it, or decide to go with something smaller, that's okay. I won't be insulted."

I hated to waste his time, but at the very least, I did need to figure out the difference between various motors and what might work best for my boat. Clearly the internet had let me down. Hopefully Andy's information would be sounder.

Andy turned and showed me the first motor, telling me a bunch of technical information that meant nothing to me. All I got out of it was that the motor was fifty horsepower. The next one was one-hundred-fifteen horsepower, and the last one was one-hundred-seventy-five. Any nuanced differences between the three were lost on me. Then Andy told me the prices and I just about fainted.

Actually, I almost burst into tears.

I don't know why I thought I'd be able to run the pontoon boat safely with something only costing a few hundred dollars, but that's what I'd come here expecting. Maybe I should have asked Andy for his prices before I set up this meeting. Or maybe I should have done more research. I frantically did the math, estimating my checking account balance after this month's bills were paid, wondering what I might be able to push off until next week's revenues came in. I had deposits for the next few months of reservations, but I hated to dip into that pool of money. If people cancelled up to three days before their reservation, I'd need to refund their deposit. Few people cancelled, but I still hated to count on that money, let alone use it to buy a motor.

Could I get by with a five or six hundred dollar motor? I didn't want something breaking down all the time. Downtime while I got it fixed would be a problem, and having the motor stop working while I was out in the middle of the lake with guests would be disastrous. I needed something that I could rely on, that would get me and my guests safely back and forth from our excursions. I couldn't afford to have cancelled events because of a maintenance issue, or have my guests paddling or swimming for the shore because we were stranded.

I got the feeling this was one of those circumstances where spending more money than I'd planned was the smart thing to do.

Andy glance between the two of us, then jerked his thumb toward the house. "I'm going to go in and make sure Xanadu is not up on the kitchen counters with her nose in the breadbox. You all talk, and I'll be back out in a few minutes."

Andy went inside and Jake turned to me. "You've got a twenty-foot pontoon boat, so you definitely don't want to get anything under fifty horsepower."

I tried not to hyperventilate. "That sounds kinda big." They all sounded big. And way more expensive than I'd expected to pay.

"It's *actually* rather small for your boat, but lots of lakes have horsepower restrictions. The engine does a lot of the work on pontoon boats as opposed to on something with a monohull, and you have to take into consideration the speed you're aiming for as well as the weight of the boat fully loaded with people. I'm thinking you'll probably be able to carry twelve on the boat at a maximum. Honestly, it would probably be a better experience with no more than eight, but that's my opinion. Keep in mind that with six or eight guests and a fifty horsepower motor, you might not be able to go much faster than the equivalent of ten miles per hour."

I tried to figure out how fast that was. My drive had a ten mile-per-hour speed limit, and that seemed plenty fast on a gravel drive in a car. Was ten miles per hour fast or slow in a boat? And didn't people call the speed knots or something? Although if Jake had used knots, or knots-per-hour, or whatever, I wouldn't have had any idea at all what he was talking about.

"I think that might be too slow. I want a leisurely ride, but not *super* leisurely. I'm worried it will take us forever to get anywhere at that speed."

He nodded. "Savage Lake doesn't have any speed restrictions—not that you want to go tearing around in a pontoon boat with a bunch of guests, but it'll play into the engine size you want to get. I'd suggest an absolute minimum of ninety horsepower. Bigger is always better. Not crazy big, but big enough that if you need to rush back to beat a storm, you can."

"So what do you recommend?" I asked, feeling absolutely unable to make this decision on my own and very appreciative that Jake had offered to help.

"Me? I'd go with the one-seventy-five, but I like to err on the side of caution. If you end up with a dozen people plus coolers with drinks and food, and you need to hustle back to the dock, you won't be panicking if you've got the one-seventy-five."

I was so confused about all this. Pivoting, I pointed to the third motor Andy had shown us. "So, this one?"

He nodded.

I bit my lip, once more mentally examining my checking account and tabulating the other bills I needed to pay this month. "That's the one he said was fifty-five hundred."

The smaller one was two grand, and that extra thirty-five

hundred was a significant cost for me. But if I could charge thirty per person for the sunset cruise and run it twice a week with ten guests, I'd make enough to cover the cost of the larger motor in four months. Then the October and early November cruises would be pure profit.

"It's going to last more than one year, right?" I asked Jake, feeling a bit of a fool about the question. "I mean, it's a used motor. I don't know what to expect in terms of lifespan, and if I need to replace it next spring, it might not be worth it for me."

"A new one would be twelve or thirteen grand," Jake pointed out. "You can ask Andy to guarantee it for thirty days. Honestly it looks to be in good condition. Andy's good with engine repair. With some basic maintenance there's no reason you can't get another five to ten years out of this motor."

That made me feel a lot better, especially because I knew a teenager I could pay to do the regular maintenance.

"Give me a minute," I told him. Then I went outside and called Mom.

"It's fifty-five hundred dollars," I blurted out when she answered. "There is a smaller ones I could go with, but Jake said if I had a dozen guests on board with coolers and drinks and everything, and we needed to get back to beat a storm, the small motor might not get us there."

Mom whistled. "That's a lot of money. Do you think we'll have that many guests interested in the lake cruises?"

"I do. The surveys I've done showed that people love the idea of the sunset cruise with champagne, and enough people showed interest in the history cruises that I think we can run one a week. People come here not just to hike, but to enjoy the lake, and what better way to enjoy the lake than on a boat?"

"We do rent out canoes and kayaks," Mom pointed out.

"Yes, but this would be different. Some people don't feel comfortable taking a canoe or kayak out. This way they could enjoy the lake without having to paddle themselves. It's a more luxurious experience." Not that a pontoon boat was all that luxurious, but compared to a kayak, it sort of was.

"Is it something that can wait for a few months?" Mom asked.

I thought about that a second. "We've got a short window to make money with this boat before the season is over. If I wait a few months to buy a motor, then I might as well wait for next year. Yeah, I'll be able to book sunset cruises, history cruises and ghost tours through the fall, but we won't have the volume of guests that we do in the summer, and not all of them will be staying for a whole week, so it limits the number of potential customers."

"Do you have the money?"

That was the big question—the most important of all the questions.

"Yes, but we'll be really tight. It'll take a few months to earn back enough to cover the cost of the motor. If we have a horrible disaster in the next thirty or even sixty days, I won't have a cushion to draw from. I might not have enough to deal with the emergency."

That was my fear. If the fridge in the camp store went, another storm washed the driveway out again, a tree fell on one of the cabins, our well pump failed, or the septic system blew up on us, I'd be in trouble.

"If there's a disaster, I can help." Mom cut me off as I started to protest. "I don't get a lot in my social security payments, and most of that goes for my supplemental medical and prescription plans, but I've been able to save some money over the last few years."

"Mom, I can't rely on you to bail out my business with your savings," I said.

ELVIS FINDS A BONE

She made a "psh" sound. "It's *our* business. And I'm looking forward to going out on these sunset cruises myself. If it really bothers you, then call it a loan."

I did the math again, and once more nearly had a panic attack. But there were risks in every business. It all came down to two choices—buy the motor and market the heck out of these cruises to make them pay for themselves as quickly as possible, or don't buy the motor, save up to purchase one next year, and come up with other ideas to make extra cash from the campground.

"Thanks, Mom," I told her. Then I disconnected the call and walked back into the garage, still undecided.

"What do you think?" Jake asked.

I took a deep breath and slowly let it out, calming the panic of spending this much money all at once. "I'm going to do it."

"I'll get the one-seventy-five." I told Andy when he came back out. "As long as you'll guarantee that it's going to not break down in the next sixty days," I amended.

"I'll guarantee mechanical function, but if you run it into some rocks or bang it up loading onto a trailer, you're on your own. Is that fair?" Andy said.

"More than fair." I got my checkbook out while Jake went to lower his truck tailgate and pull a bunch of rope and bungie cords out of the back of the cab.

Andy took my check, teasing me that he knew where I lived if it bounced. Then he flipped the locks on the stand's wheels and pushed the whole apparatus out to the rear of Jakes truck. Using a lever on the side of the stand, he raised the motor to where the larger, and I presumed heavier, section was above the tailgate. Jake hopped into the back as Andy unlatched the motor, and the two of them guided it onto the tailgate.

The truck's back end sagged noticeably, making me

wonder if Jake, Austin, and his friends would be able to get the thing out of the truck bed and onto the boat without anyone suffering a hernia.

Andy jumped into the back of the truck. He and Jake carefully maneuvered the motor into the center of the bed, then secured it to the tie-down loops. When they were satisfied that the motor was safe for transport, they both hopped out. I shook Andy's hand and thanked him while Jake closed the tailgate. Then we climbed into the truck and left Andy with one less motor and fifty-five hundred dollars richer.

"Thank you," I said as we pulled out of the development. "If you hadn't helped, I would have ended up stranded in the middle of the lake with a dozen guests and a motor that wouldn't power more than a blender."

He laughed. "I'm glad I could be of service. Have you eaten yet?"

I blinked at the unexpected question. "No. Mom and I usually eat around six or seven. We didn't fix anything special since I wasn't sure how long I'd be at Andy's. Did you want to join us for leftover minestrone and roast beef sandwiches?"

"I was thinking we could eat out—unless your mom is expecting you back."

I pondered that for a few seconds, not sure if he was offering to go through a fast-food drive-through, or meant a sit-down meal. Honestly, either one sounded good to me. I was hungry, and as yummy as the roast beef and leftover minestrone seemed early today, the thought of putting together a sandwich and warming up soup felt beyond my abilities right now.

"Mom is fine on her own," I told him. "Plus, Austin is there until eight to help out, and Tuesday isn't a busy day for us. That's why it's normally my day off."

He glanced over at me, then looked back at the road. "Any

food preferences? Allergies? I'm guessing you're not vegetarian if you were planning on roast beef sandwiches."

I shook my head. "No allergies or preferences. I'll try anything as long as it's not trying to walk off my plate."

He chuckled. "Well, the steaks at the Chat-n-Chew are probably still mooing if you order them rare, and I'll totally judge you if you order them well done."

I smiled. "Judge? Or arrest me?"

"Judge." He laughed. "Well-done steaks aren't quite the crime of pineapple on pizza."

"They are in my opinion," I teased. "Steaks sound good. So...Chat-n-Chew?"

I'd never eaten there. Hopefully we wouldn't need a reservation, although it seemed few places in Reckless needed reservations.

"Chat-n-Chew it is," Jake confirmed. "Hope you've got your eating pants on, because the servings are huge."

CHAPTER 14

*T*he Chat-n-Chew wasn't five star, but it was the closest thing to fine dining that the town of Reckless had to offer, and it was packed with diners. Booths lined three walls, with shiny burgundy fake-leather bench seats and tables with plastic wood-grain tops. Four and two seated tables stood in rows in the center of the restaurant. Those tables were the same as the ones in the booths, but the chairs were chrome-covered aluminum with black vinyl seat cushions. The double doors and pass-through to the kitchen were beside a bar with stools for eight patrons.

In the center of each table was a plastic caddy with salt, pepper, ketchup, hot sauce, steak sauce, and malt vinegar. The waitstaff bustled about, their outfits something I could only describe as French maid meets yoga instructor.

"Deputy Jake!"

A woman hustled up to us in black leggings, black jogging shoes, and a frilly white blouse. An equally frilly apron was tied around her waist. It had pockets that held a pad for taking orders, and about a dozen pens. I stared at the apron then at the frilly blouse, wondering if the Chat-n-Chew only hired women for their waitstaff, or if they required the men to wear the same outfit.

"We didn't call ahead, Paula. Can you squeeze us in some-where?" Jake smiled at her and I could swear that the woman blushed.

"Of course! Ray Potts is just getting ready to leave. Let me hustle him along, give his table a quick wipe, and I'll have you seated in a jiffy."

"Don't rush Ray on our account," Jake quickly said before the woman could dash off.

She waved a hand. "Oh, that man needs to be rushed, otherwise he'll sit there sipping water all night and taking up valuable real estate. He finished dinner and paid his bill a half hour ago. The man needs to go home."

We watched Paula leave, then Jake turned to me, leaning close. "Ray doesn't want to go home, because his wife has a to-do list a mile long."

I looked up at him. "Are you saying his wife's a nag?"

Jake chuckled. "I'm saying that Ray is lazy. Pru won't get anything done around the house if she doesn't staple that list to his forehead and remind him of it every five minutes. The guy spends all day either fishing or down at the Bait and Beer playing games. He certainly can get off his butt and take the trash to the curb."

"That's very enlightened of you, Deputy Jake," I teased.

Ray Potts wasn't inclined to leave just yet, but as the hostess spoke to him, another couple who'd been seated a few booths down got up. They exchanged pleasantries with Jake as they left and I watched while three of the staff descended on the booth to grab dirty dishes and wipe it down with cleaning products. A few minutes later, the hostess was escorting us to the booth.

I slid onto the bench seat, across from Jake. A young woman who looked to be in her late teens with what was clearly the Chat-n-Chew's signature uniform approached and put two bundles of napkin-wrapped silverware in front of each of us, then handed us each a menu.

"Can I get y'all something to drink?" She beamed alternately at Jake and me while I quickly glanced at the menu.

"Unsweet tea, please," I said after seeing that my choices were tea, coffee, or Coke products.

"Sweet tea for me, Nikki." Jake smiled up at her. "How is your dad doing?"

Nikki's smile widened. "Good, thanks. It's been a busy summer for him with all the dry weather."

"Nikki's dad, Viktor, is one of our volunteer firefighters here in Reckless, " Jake explained. "The day he retires will be a sad day for the town."

Nikki snorted. "Retire. He'll be out there at ninety with his walker still pulling hoses. Ben's thinking of joining up, though. So even if Dad retires, there will still be a Norman fighting fires in Reckless."

Nikki left with our drink order and I watched her go, thinking she'd probably gone to high school with Austin.

"If you're looking to bring on additional help at the campground, I can recommend Nikki," Jake said. "She did some barn help for me last summer. She's a hard worker."

"Will she be going to college in the fall?" I did need some additional help, especially if Austin was going to be driving the pontoon boat for me, but I was hoping to hire someone who might be able to continue on at least through the end of September.

"I remember Viktor told me she was going to do a few years at the community college in Derwood, then maybe transfer to a four year once she figured out what she wanted to major in." Jake smiled. "So she'll be around for two years at least."

"I'll ask her if she's available." I did need the extra help, but I was also really short on cash after buying a motor so I wasn't sure how many hours per week I could promise the girl.

Nikki returned, sat our drinks down, then pulled a pen and pad out of a pocket in her apron. "Do y'all know what you want to eat?

"I'll have the Sheriff Special," I told her, half teasing.

"Oh, I'm so sorry ma'am. We are sold out of prime rib tonight. The Reckless Angler Society finished up their meeting early and descended on us like a pack of locusts. Ate us clean out of prime rib."

Was it funny or not funny that she knew exactly what I was talking about when I requested the Sheriff Special?

"The Porterhouse is really good here," Jake mentioned.

"And lots of people order the stuffed flounder," Nikki added. "Our fish and the crab meat come from a supplier on the shore. It's not that frozen, chain-distributor stuff. And the steaks are all local beef from Savage Butchers."

I wasn't sure whether having meat from "Savage" Butchers was any better than "Reckless" Butchers, but amusing town names aside, I was sure the food was good. Jake was nodding in agreement with our waitress, and clearly the sheriff was well on his way to a heart attack from all the red meat he ate here.

"I'll take the stuffed flounder," I told her, making a mental note to come back early one evening with Mom so we could try the legendary prime rib. "With the grilled asparagus and rice pilaf, please."

Jake ordered the Porterhouse with a loaded baked potato and cheesy broccoli, making me fear for his cholesterol levels, then we fell once again into that silence as Nikki left with our order and our menus.

It didn't feel as awkward as it had in the truck. Still, this was the *Chat*-n-Chew, and I felt we should keep with the theme.

"I'm wondering why you weren't at the Reckless Angler Club meeting. If you'd have attended, you would have been here in time to score some prime rib."

"That's the Reckless Angler *Society*," he corrected me with a grin. "And I had something more important to do. I was helping my friend purchase a motor for her pontoon boat."

I'd been teasing, but now I felt bad that he'd missed the meeting. "Jake! We could have met Andy tomorrow. You didn't have to skip your club on my behalf."

"Trust me, I would rather be with you looking at used motors than sitting at the Community Center with twelve men discussing lures and reels. I belong because every now and then someone brings beer. Then they get drunk and spill the goods on their secret fishing spots. I stay sober and know where to go the next day."

I bit back a smile. "And they don't chase you off? I assumed you anglers would be possessive about your secret fishing spots."

Jake leaned back and wiggled his eyebrows. "I'm a part-time, on-call deputy. You seriously think they'd chase me off?"

I laughed. "Well, don't hog all the trout, or whatever it is you catch, for yourself. Leave some in the lake for the rest of us."

He gave me an odd look. "Do you like trout? I mostly get walleye, bass, or yellow perch."

"I'd be happy to score *any* of those. I can't seem to catch anything besides sticks and sludge on my hook. I've been out fishing twice so far, and it's clear I have no talent for this sport."

"There's no need for big talent in fishing, there's patience, persistence, and a willingness to learn and try different things. If you just want to enjoy some quiet time on a boat with a line in the water, then don't worry about what comes up on your hook. But if you actually want to catch fish, then you need to do some learning about bait and lures and casting techniques as well as ideal fishing spots."

I puffed my cheeks and blew out a breath. "That sounds like too much work. Can I just putz around in on the lake and have someone bring me fish? Preferably already dressed and fileted, because I have no idea how to do any of that."

It wasn't that I was lazy, or that I didn't appreciate the work that went into catching fish. I was so busy with the campground, so overwhelmed with my new business, that I needed my hobbies to be restful. Like sitting on the dock with a book, or hiking with Elvis, or enjoying a cup of coffee or a glass of wine with my friends.

Or solving a murder.

"Tell you what. If I bring in more than one fish, I'll filet it and gift it to you as part of my payment for letting me use your slip."

He had already offered to give me some of his venison from this year's hunting season, claiming that he always had too much for him to eat by himself, and now he was offering me fish.

"Or you can filet both fish, bring them by, and let me cook them for us," I offered. "I'm not a gourmet chef or anything, but I'm a pretty decent cook."

He hesitated, and I wondered if I'd gone too far. We were friends, but with any friendship of heterosexual individuals of opposite genders, we were walking that fine line. We were dancing around the divide between friendship and more, and for some weird reason, I couldn't help push that boundary every now and then.

"Sure." His voice had some odd note to it, like he was

staring at an apple handed to him by Eve and wondering if he dared eat it or not. "That would be...nice."

I switched the conversation to the weather, probably to both of our relief. Then when our food arrived, we did lapse into silence as we enjoyed our meals.

The flounder was really good. As was the crab-meat stuffing. It was past asparagus season in this area, but the tender shoots, grilled and coated in butter, tasted farm fresh. And the rice pilaf was Basmati and cooked with chicken stock, saffron, and sliced almonds. None of the food was particularly fancy, but I ended the meal more satisfied than I'd been after eating at some of the high-end Michelin-rated restaurants I'd gone to in my corporate days.

As we ate, Nikki stopped by a few times to refill our drinks. I talked to her about the campground, and ask if she'd be interested in working at the camp store a few days a week —either during the day or early evenings when we'd be taking groups out on the boat. She seemed excited about the prospect and wrote down my name and number, promising to stop by in the next day or two and discuss the job in more detail.

I felt a little guilty poaching an employee while dining at the Chat-n-Chew, and told her so.

She waved that away with a smile. "Aww, I'm only filling in here while Sarah's on vacation. I promised to fill in for Joy Ann over July 4th week, but other than that, I'm available to work elsewhere."

She'd pointed at a slim raven-haired waitress as she'd spoke and I blinked in surprise. "That's Joy Ann? Do you think she'd have a minute to talk to me?"

Lottie and I had planned to come by and ask Joy Ann questions about Buddy over the next few days, but I figured I might take advantage of the opportunity. Plus with Jake here, she might be more inclined to answer my questions.

"Sure. Her shift is ending soon, so they're not seating her any more tables. I'll see if she'll come over." Nikki hesitated. "Are you going to hire her, too?"

I might as well be honest.

"I didn't plan on it. I wanted to ask her about a man she used to date—Buddy Hooper."

CHAPTER 15

*T*he name didn't elicit a particularly strong reaction from Nikki, but when the girl asked Joy Ann to come talk to me I saw the woman glance over at me with a frown.

"Joy Ann? Buddy?" Jake asked with raised eyebrows.

"Yes, Joy Ann. Buddy. I'm being nosy again," I told him. "Actually, both Lottie and I are being nosy. We figured that we'd look into the man's disappearance. It's not like we're interfering with an open police investigation or anything."

"No, although that's never stopped you and Lottie in the past," he said with a laugh.

I hushed him, smiling as I saw Joy Ann made her way over to our table.

She nodded to Jake, then turned to face me. "You're the campground woman. Nikki said you wanted to talk about Buddy Hooper?"

"Yes, I did," I said. "Someone told me you used to date Buddy Hooper and I wondered if I could ask you a few questions about him."

"Date is probably a strong word when it came to Buddy

and me." Her smile faded and she turned to Jake. "Everyone's saying the body that turned up in the woods by Beal's Gap was his. Is it true?"

"We don't know who it is yet," Jake said. "It might have been a lost hiker, or a hunter killed by accident, or even a suicide. There's no sense in speculating until we have more information and until Stef completes the autopsy."

I noticed he didn't say anything about the man being shot in the head. I was surprised that wasn't all over town by now since most of the Reckless Sniffer's Club had been there when Stef had excavated the remains.

"I know, it's just been so long since Buddy left, and no one's heard anything about him." Joy's mouth trembled a bit. "We weren't anything serious, but I saw him once or twice a week those last few months. He told me up front that he had some big deal going on, and that he might move out of town soon, but I always assumed he'd be back here and there for a…visit."

"Is that why you didn't immediately report him missing?" I asked the woman.

She nodded. "It threw me a bit when he just up and left without any warning, especially since we were supposed to meet up that Tuesday, but Buddy wasn't the kind of guy who was in the habit of being accountable to anyone. And he was notorious for ghosting on a girl. If you got a text cancelling a hookup you were lucky. It didn't bother me any. I knew we were just casual and temporary. I know it bothered some women, though."

"Like who?" I asked, wondering if Buddy's disappearance had anything to do with a jealous, spurned lover.

"Not that I want to out anyone," she said before proceeding to do just that, "but Ellen Preston for one. She got a little stalkery when Buddy stopped seeing her. Seems she thought they had something long-term and serious going on. Then there was Marcie Boarding. Not that Marcie wanted a boyfriend or a second husband, but she did want Buddy to be at her beck and call twenty-four-seven."

"Can you tell me about the last time you saw Buddy?" I asked.

She knotted her fingers together, looked down at them, then back up at me. "It was a Friday. I remember because I don't normally get off on Fridays and I was excited to not be working. We ordered pizza. Buddy brought over some beer. Then we...you know."

Yes, I knew, and I didn't want any of *those* details.

"He couldn't spend the night because he had to be up super early for a hauling job," Joy Ann continued. "He had a lot of hauling jobs the months we were seeing each other. Sometimes it interfered with his hay delivery schedules, but Buddy said the hauling jobs came first because they were the big money."

I frowned, wondering again if that accounted for the extra deposits I'd seen in Buddy's checking account. But hadn't Buddy always done some hauling here and there? I didn't know much about the pay for those kinds of jobs, but I couldn't believe some extra hauling gigs could account for tens of thousands of extra income.

"He left that night, and I never saw him again." Joy Ann frowned in thought. "It was the first week in June. I didn't really think anything about it that week since Buddy sometimes got busy and didn't always return texts. Even when he stood me up on Tuesday, I figured he forgot or something came up and he just didn't let me know. But when I hadn't heard anything from him in two weeks, I called the Sheriff."

My eyes widened and I turned to Jake. "I thought no one reported him missing until sometime in July?"

He nodded, then looked over at Joy Ann. "You called mid-June and said he was missing?"

Joy Ann shifted her weight from foot to foot. "I did. The sheriff came out and said that this was what Buddy did to women, and that I shouldn't take it personally. He said Buddy probably decided he was done with me and that I should just move on."

I caught my breath, hating our sheriff even more. What a callous thing to say to someone, even if it might have been true. But it clearly wasn't true. I didn't know if Buddy ran off voluntarily or was killed, but one thing everyone agreed upon was that he'd gone missing sometime in June and had never been seen in Reckless again.

"I'm so sorry, Joy Ann," Jake told her. "That wasn't right what the sheriff said to you. He should have taken your concerns seriously and looked into them. I'm sorry he treated you like that."

I eyed Jake in surprise, not sure if even a sometimes-deputy was supposed to be criticizing his boss—even if it was valid criticism.

"Thank you." Joy Ann nodded to him, then faced me again. "Anyway, I never saw Buddy again. I thought about what the sheriff said, and knew he wasn't wrong. And then there was the fact that Buddy had been talking about some big business deal that would cause him to move away. I tried to just put him out of my mind, but when I hadn't heard anything by the end of July, and I found out that no one else had seen or heard from him, I called again. This time I spoke to Deputy Sean and he opened a missing person report. Not that a missing person report did anything to find Buddy."

I waited for Jake to give his spiel about missing people who wanted to be missing and that adults had the right to run off, but he remained silent.

"Any idea what this big business deal was about?" I asked Joy Ann, thinking about the increase in deposits over the last six months Buddy had been around.

She shook her head. "I don't know who he was hauling for, but I got the idea it was always the same company. Like he had some kind of exclusive contract or something. I do remember him saying he needed to go pick up a rental trailer —a big flatbed one. He had to go all the way to Derwood to get it from Big Rigs Rentals because the ones for rent in Reckless were too small. He was complaining about picking it up super early in the morning and then having to backtrack to drive to Roanoke for the haul pickup, but he didn't want to get the trailer the night before and have to pay an extra day's rental. That's all I know."

"One more thing," I said as she turned to leave. "Was Buddy buying overstock electronics and reselling them for a profit?"

She frowned. "No, but I think maybe that was some perk of this hauling job. He gave me a brand-new cell phone in April—that model hadn't even hit the stores yet. Just casually gave it to me like that thing wasn't worth seven or eight hundred dollars at least. I figured maybe it was a demo model that they send to stores that he managed to get his hands on. But that was it. I don't remember him buying or selling electronics. Buddy farmed and hauled. He wasn't the tech sort, if you get what I mean."

I watched her go, even more confused. A demo phone given to him as a perk for his hauling job made sense. But multiple cell phones, a laptop, a gaming computer, and a really expensive GPS collar? Those weren't casual gifts or perks.

Had he stolen them? I thought about Buddy's hauling job, the big deposits of cash, and began to wonder about the man's side job.

CHAPTER 16

"*D*idn't you have any questions you wanted to ask Joy Ann?" I asked Jake as the woman headed back toward the kitchen to pick up a food order.

He'd had an odd expression on his face when Joy Ann had talked about Buddy's hauling job, the trailer, and the cell phone. It made me wonder what was going through his head, and what the significance of all that might be. Buddy had done hauling before. Was it that the job was in Roanoke? Was it that the trailer needed to be picked up in Derwood? Was it the size of the trailer?

Or was it the cell phone? Could Jake be thinking that Buddy was a thief? Because that's exactly what I was thinking.

Jake shook his head. "Nope. No questions. I'm off duty. Besides, I already questioned her and some of the other women Buddy was known to be seeing when he vanished last year. I see the wheels turning in your head, but none of those women has any real motive to see Buddy dead."

"So you do admit he's dead," I said.

He sighed. "I'm not admitting anything right now. Like I

told you before, sometimes people get in over their heads in debt and run out of town. An adult has the perfect right to take off and leave everything behind if they want to."

"But Buddy wasn't actually in debt," I countered. "Yes, he was behind on his rent and Tony Marconi was evicting him, and if he had some big business deal that would take him out of town, he might have wanted to just stiff Tony. But the guy had money, Jake. He had thirty grand in his checking account according to his May statement from last year. And he'd paid off both his truck and his tractor in May. That was around eighteen grand. So if he left voluntarily, it wasn't to run out on debts."

"*Thirty grand* in his checking account?" Jake stared at me, all sorts of unreadable expressions flashing across his face. "Wait…how the heck do you know what Buddy's checking account balance was or that he paid off his car and tractor?"

"Ellen Preston bought the contents of Buddy's storage unit when it went to auction this past January, and she's kept it in her back room for the last six months. There was a box with his personal papers and his bank statements."

I didn't tell him about Mom looking into Buddy's credit report. No sense in getting my own mother in trouble with the law. Although I was pretty sure Jake wouldn't go arresting her, he certainly wouldn't be happy about her hacking activities.

"So he didn't leave for debts." Jake gave an exaggerated shrug. "He might have had a big job offer out of state like Joy Ann said. Leaving town without telling everyone your forwarding address isn't against the law, Sassy."

"But where did all the money come from?" I asked him. "In six months Buddy managed to increase his checking account balance by thirty grand, and somehow come up with the cash to pay off his truck and his tractor. That's a lot of hay to farm and sell, all in six months."

Jake shrugged once more. "Okay. Maybe Buddy was involved in something illegal."

"And then he goes missing," I added.

"If he was involved in something illegal, he might have had a good reason to go missing," Jake pointed out.

He was right. But thirty grand wasn't enough to hide out on an island for the rest of your life. It wasn't run-away-from-the-mob kind of money. But it was enough money for someone to get killed over. If Buddy had double-crossed a partner in something illegal, or was blackmailing someone, then he might be dead. He might be that body Elvis found in the woods.

The money. If Buddy had run off with some ill-gotten gains then he would have taken those gains with him. The last bank statement I had was May's. If that account had been cleared out, then Jake was right and he probably was alive. But if it was still in his checking account for over a year, then Buddy had probably been killed before he could withdraw the funds.

Could Mom hack into a bank? I took a sip of my tea and eyed Jake. He could probably get a warrant for the account records, but to do that he'd need to have some solid proof that Buddy had committed a crime or was dead. I was sure that would be his next step if Stef identified the body as Buddy's, but that might take weeks or even months, where Mom might be able to check the account balance within hours.

"It's the electronics," I told him. "Ellen said when she bought the storage unit, there was an expensive gaming computer, a laptop, and several cell phones—all of them new and in the box. Then there's that cell phone he gave Joy Ann. Oh, and there was a brand-new GPS tracking collar in the box with all his bank statements. It hadn't even been opened yet. I've been shopping around for one, and that model retails for around fifteen hundred dollars."

Jake frowned. "Does Ellen still have the electronics?"

"No. She said Mike Allen offered her two thousand dollars for it all right there at the auction so she sold it to him. She said she doesn't really deal in used electronics. I've still got the tracking collar, though."

Jake sat in silence for a few minutes, lost in thought. When he finally looked up at me, he had that hard, cop-look in his eyes that never failed to make me feel as if I were guilty of something.

"Can I see the GPS collar after we get the motor on your boat? And I need to ask you not to open the package or give it or any of the contents of those boxes to anyone—at least for a few days."

"Sure." I eyed him. "It all belongs to Ellen, though, so you should probably talk to her if you need to take possession of everything. Lottie has two boxes as well, but I don't know what, if anything, she's found in them."

"Right now I just want you and Lottie to keep everything together."

"If Buddy was stealing electronics from somewhere and reselling them," I said, throwing my theory out there, "then maybe his partner and he had a falling out. The partner kills Buddy, and buries his body in the woods."

"Or Buddy was involved in some illegal activity involving stolen electronics. Things got too hot, so he took off out of town before they got caught and he could be arrested," Jake amended.

If that was the case, then Buddy would have emptied his checking account before leaving. He'd want all the money he could grab to ensure he stayed off the radar of both his former partners and the police. If the money was still in the checking account, then I'd assume Buddy was dead. If it had been cleaned out last year, then I'd assume Jake's theory was right.

"Since the town is buzzing with rumors, Stef went ahead and asked for Buddy's dental records," Jake said, interrupting my thoughts. "The DNA will take weeks at best, and we don't have any of Buddy's to compare it to, so she's going to compare Buddy's dental records to the teeth on the body. That should either put the rumors to rest, or give us enough that we can look closer into what happened to Buddy Hooper last year."

"Any idea on when Steff will get those dental records?" I asked.

Jake shrugged. "Normally she gets them in the next day, but since we don't have a warrant and there are some privacy hoops to jump through, it's taking longer. She thinks she'll have them by Thursday or Friday at the latest."

That wasn't so bad.

"If Buddy *was* involved in something shady, who do you think his partner might have been?" I asked Jake. "And who might want him dead?"

Jake's expression was blank as he replied. "I've got no idea."

I narrowed my eyes, pretty sure that Jake was lying. He did have ideas; he just wasn't willing to share them with me.

"How about Marcus LaSalle?" I asked. "He sued Buddy over something last year. Maybe Buddy's death wasn't connected to the electronics stuff, but over that lawsuit."

Jake shook his head. "I can't see that. The lawsuit was over some puppies and a stud fee for Marcus's dog. He and Buddy ended up agreeing on a settlement amount. It was only five hundred dollars, Sassy. And Buddy paid him. I can't see Marcus killing Buddy over a disagreement that was settled. Plus, Marcus resolves all his disputes through lawsuits, not violence."

Jake flagged down Nikki for the check, redirecting any further attempts to talk about Buddy or the body. We had a brief tussle over who was going to pay the check, and he won with me insisting on at least covering the tip.

We made it back to the campground before Austin had left for the day. He and Jake somehow managed to get the heavy motor from his truck onto the back of the pontoon boat. The sun was setting as he and Austin launched the boat, started up the motor, and gave it a quick test run before tying it up in the slip across from Jake's fishing boat.

"Seems seaworthy," Jake told me once he and Austin had finished securing the boat. "Make sure you have Austin or someone else who's familiar with boats out on the first few trips, just in case there's a problem."

"Austin's my captain until I can take some boating classes and get my license," I told Jake. "And I plan to make the first trip friends-only, just to work out any kinks before we start taking paying customers out."

"That's a good plan." He smiled. "Can I see that GPS collar real quick? Then I need to get going so I can turn the horses out to pasture for the night."

"Of course!"

I led Jake to the house. He petted Elvis and chatted with Mom while I got the collar. As he snapped pictures and wrote down the information from the back of the package, I e-mailed him the spreadsheets I'd put together with Buddy's deposits and withdrawals.

"Holy cow," he said as he glanced at the spreadsheets. "How long did this take you?"

"Not long," I lied, not wanting to let him know that I'd spend pretty much my entire day off on it.

"Well, you could be an analyst if you ever get tired of running the campground." He laughed at my horrified expression. "I'll deny I ever said this, but I'm glad you and

Lottie decided to dig your nosy-noses into Buddy's disappearance. It's too early to say for sure, but I think you two may have unearthed some valuable clues."

I beamed, excited that our amateur sleuthing may have helped solve a crime. "Thank you for all your help tonight with the motor. And for dinner. See you tomorrow? In the morning when you go fishing, I mean?" I hastily amended.

"Absolutely," he said as he walked toward the door. "See you tomorrow."

CHAPTER 17

I woke up to another beautiful, sunny morning on Wednesday. The weather had been glorious this summer, but the lack of rain was taking its toll on local farmers and on the lake which had dropped in volume. The drought wasn't bad enough that we could see the rooftops of houses flooded to create the lake a hundred years ago, but I'd been told the marshy areas of the lake were turning to mud in sections, and that might threaten some of the plants and animals that called those marshes home.

Jake did not come fishing.

I kept glancing out the window as I made coffee, organized Flora's food delivery, and helped customers, but I didn't see the familiar truck pulling down the driveway. When I looked out the door at nine, his boat still floated at the end of the dock, tied to the slip.

At first I shrugged it off, thinking that he might have been called up for some deputy job, or that maybe those dental records had come in and he was neck-deep in work with that murder case. Then weird insidious doubts crept up and burrowed into my mind. Maybe he was avoiding me. Was last night too date-y? Had I said something that made him think I was interested in him as more than a friend? After a night of reflection, had he decided to put some distance between us and cool our friendship? Would I wake up tomorrow to find his boat gone and that he was now using the public launch for the rest of the summer?

I didn't call or text, and I shoved those thoughts into a little box and locked them away. I was a grown woman, not some teen with a crush. Jake was probably working. End of story.

Instead, I texted Lottie, letting her know that we needed to update each other on our sleuthing. I had new information for her, and if Jake was following a lead today, there was a good chance Lottie would know about it through her information network.

Then I put the "be back later" sign on the door, walked Elvis, and gave a little prayer for rain. Not like the storm that washed out part of my driveway, but a gentle cool rain. At night. When campers would be sleeping and not having to postpone plans.

Ellie and Allie came by at eight to play more hide-and-seek with Elvis. I had them take Elvis off with his new GPS collar so I was the one doing the tracking this time, locating him easily with the handheld remote. Happy that the collar worked as advertised, I let the girls play with the hound on their own. They'd be leaving tomorrow afternoon, and I knew they'd miss Elvis as much as he'd miss them. I checked on them occasionally out the window as I worked, making sure one of the girls had the end of the hound's long, forty-foot leash.

Nikki from the Chat-n-Chew stopped by around ten, just when Mom had arrived to take over at the camp store. I showed the girl around the campground, then Mom and I went over the various things she would need to do in the camp store on her shifts.

"I can only promise you about ten to fifteen hours a week right now," I warned her. "If these cruises take off, I could probably give you additional hours until the end of summer though."

She accepted the offer and I told her that I'd see her starting Monday. Nikki was just pulling out of the parking area when Lottie pulled in.

"Have I got news for you," she said as she climbed the steps.

"Me too. Come in and have some coffee. Mom needs an update as well."

We went inside, got our drinks, and sat at the little café table with Elvis snoozing at our feet.

"Did you find anything in your boxes?" Lottie asked in between sips of her coffee.

"There wasn't a smoking gun, but I did find a few things that gave me pause." I told her about the increase in deposits, and the large amount of money in Buddy's checking account when he'd gone missing as well as the payoffs of both his truck and his tractor loans. Then I told her about the GPS collar.

"He sure had a lot of new, unopened electronics sitting around," Lottie pointed out.

I nodded. "And he evidently gave Joy Ann a brand-new cell phone. The thing wasn't even on the shelves yet. She thought maybe he'd gotten it as a perk from one of his hauling jobs, but the guy had a ton of new electronics. No one gets that many freebies. I'm thinking he was working with a partner or a group stealing and fencing electronics."

"They'd need to be working with an employee at a retail location." Mom hesitated. "Or several employees at several locations. With security cameras and tracking devices, it's not easy for employees to regularly steal that sort of high-end product."

"Maybe they did the whole 'it fell of a truck' routine," Lottie suggested. "Either hijack a shipment, or intercept it in transit and grab some or all of the product."

"Honestly it could all be done electronically without ever having to deal with snatch-and-grab, or truck hijacking," Mom said. "Set up sales and shipments using stolen credit cards and PO Boxes that were rented with fake addresses. Or if you've got someone in order entry, fulfillment, or purchasing, you could move the product then edit the records to cover it up."

I frowned. "How would that work?"

Mom sat back in her chair. "Put in four or five fake orders with Net 30 billing. Have it collected off the dock as either a pickup, or with the help of someone in shipping. Cancel the order and mark it as returned to stock. With these big companies, it wouldn't be caught until an annual inventory. And if they used a former employee's login and password, it wouldn't be traced to them. It sometimes takes weeks or even months for IT to delete an ex-employee's access, especially if they're rank-and-file workers like in order entry, or shipping."

"But how would Buddy play into that scenario?" Lottie asked. "He didn't work at a retail store or a warehouse. And he didn't have the connections to fence the stolen goods either.

"But he did have a big truck and he did hauling jobs on the side." I turned to Mom. "What if it wasn't four or five orders a month? What if it was a big shipment—big enough to fit into a box trailer?"

"That would be harder to cover up," Mom said. "Unless the company had some truly antiquated systems of record keeping, that level of theft would need to have someone in management involved to pull it off. Upper level management, probably."

"Like a VP of Purchasing?" I asked her.

Lottie gasped. "Mike Allen! He's the VP of Purchasing for Rio Grande Electronics. They've got a huge, national distribution channel with warehouses all over every state."

"A company moving that kind of volumes to lots of different places? I think a VP could cover it up, especially one in charge of purchasing or logistics or distribution. Except Rio Grande has some pretty sophisticated software. It wouldn't be easy," Mom warned.

"Mike's been there for over twenty years," Lottie said. "You work at a company that long, you get to know the weak spots."

Mom nodded. "True. They use a lot of independent trucking companies to move their product too. This Mike could set up a partner as a delivery company, finagle it so the stock was assembled to go out to a warehouse, have his partner pick it up and deliver it to a shady company or organized crime outfit to fence, then cancel the order and fudge the return-to-stock. Or he could set up a fictional warehouse for delivery. By the time the company found out, they could have stolen hundreds of thousands of dollars in goods. Or more. The big hitch would be using someone else's computer and someone else's login for the crime."

It was a solid theory, but we had absolutely no proof. Mike had bought back the electronics from the storage unit. The only items we had that might be traceable were the GPS collar and possibly Joy Ann's cell phone. But if Mike had covered his tracks, those serial numbers would show as sitting in some warehouse. Buddy would be the only one who would look like a thief—Buddy and some random former Rio Grande employee.

The other problem was that Rio Grande might not be all

that interested in what they'd assume was one or two stolen items. It probably wouldn't be worth their time to investigate that. And they'd hardly be interested in turning suspicion on an executive with twenty years of company service. We needed to find some other way to connect Mike to the electronics theft.

And we needed some way of connecting Mike to Buddy's murder—assuming the dead body *was* Buddy's.

"I've been wondering if that money is still in Buddy's account," I said. "Just because it was on that last statement doesn't mean he didn't clear out the account when he allegedly left town. If it's gone, then he's probably still alive."

"Or someone killed him and stole his ATM card," Lottie pointed out.

"True, but if it's still there, sitting in his banking account unused for a year, well we can probably assume he's dead," I finished.

"The credit report showed the checking account, but not the balance. It didn't indicate the account was closed but sometimes they don't." Mom shot me a look filled with significance. "I might be able to get into his checking account to check the balance but it would take me a few days or possibly weeks. Some banks actually have a halfway decent internet security setup."

"Ooo, let's do that." Lottie clapped. "Let's hack into his banking account."

I dug a paper out of my pocket and passed it to Mom, not in the least bit perturbed by Lottie's enthusiasm for white collar crime. "There's no need to hack into the bank, although I'm pretty sure accessing someone else's account without their permission is still technically illegal."

"Well, he's dead, so there's no one to complain," Lottie countered.

Mom took the sheet from me. "You've got to be kidding.

He actually wrote his username and password on one of his bank statements? Who does that?"

I looked away, not wanting to admit to my mother that I occasionally wrote down usernames and passwords on scrap pieces of paper as well. With all the internet shopping and bill pay nowadays, it was hard to keep track of it all—especially when you weren't supposed to use the same password for everything. I probably should get one of those internet password vault things, but for now I had sticky notes in a notebook marked "bills" on the front, super handy for any burglar to find.

Mom pulled her laptop over and got started. A few seconds later she was scrolling through Buddy Hooper's checking transactions.

"Well, the thirty grand is still there," Mom announced. "And there haven't been any transactions since June eleventh of last year. Looks like he got fuel at some place outside of Richmond using his debit card. After that, there's nothing."

A year of nothing. And thirty grand just sitting in the bank.

"Unless he found ten million in cash from a drug stash and fled the country, then I'm assuming he's dead," Lottie said. "No one abandons that much money. And no one goes an entire year without using their debit card either."

I nodded in agreement. "And his last known location was outside of Richmond. Joy Ann had said his hauling job was in Roanoke, so I'm assuming he was transporting from Roanoke to Richmond."

"Rio Grande Electronics is headquartered in Roanoke," Lottie said. "That's where their main warehouse is for the mid-Atlantic states."

"So he picked up in Roanoke, and delivered to some fencing operation in Richmond. But did he *disappear* in Richmond? Or did he make it back to Derwood to return the trailer to the rental place?" Mom asked.

"Ooo, we need to check the rental place," Lottie said, putting a quick note in her phone. "But I'm guessing he made it back to Derwood, and Reckless, otherwise his body would have been somewhere in Richmond and not in the woods near Beal's Gap."

"We should still check," Mom said. "As far as we know, no one ever saw him in Reckless after he left Joy Ann's house that night. He could have been killed outside of Richmond, and that body Elvis found in the woods could be someone else, like Jake said."

"But if he didn't return the rental trailer, wouldn't that company have come after him?" I asked. "At the very least there would have been something in Buddy's credit report saying they were suing him for a trailer he never returned. I'm guessing those things are pretty expensive."

"And if he was killed near Richmond and the trailer was just sitting on the side of the road or in a lot somewhere, it would have been reported," Lottie said. "I'm assuming it was a big trailer. Someone would have called the police about it, and it would have been traced back to the rental place and Buddy."

I frowned, thinking that the sheriff's office would have taken the missing person report a lot more seriously if the trailer was found abandoned. Or maybe not. If they thought Buddy was running out on debts, then they might also believe he wouldn't care about returning a rental trailer.

"But where's his truck?" Mom asked. "An abandoned trailer with Buddy's truck still attached would have sent up all sorts of red flags about foul play. Assuming he made it back to Derwood to return the trailer, and then to Reckless where someone killed him and disposed of his body, where is his truck? And that tractor?"

Mom was right.

"The truck is missing. The tractor is missing. If we assume he returned the trailer and that the body in the woods was Buddy's, then the truck and tractor must be somewhere around here," Mom added.

Lottie nodded. "If I'd just killed Buddy, I wouldn't want to be caught driving his truck around, but I can't imagine where a murderer would hide a big diesel pickup like that and not have *somebody* eventually see it. As far as the tractor…tons of people in this county have farms and tractors. I doubt it was so distinctive that a passerby would say 'hey, that's Buddy Hooper's tractor.'"

"So we need to verify that the trailer was returned." Mom ticked the items off on her fingers. "And think about where a killer might hide a fairly distinctive truck."

"And prove that Buddy and Mike Allen were involved in an electronics theft ring," I added. "Mike is on the top of my list as a murder suspect as well, although there might have also been a third partner who did it."

"We can't exactly confront Mike," Lottie said. "But maybe one of Buddy's lady friends knew more about his business than they've admitted. We could talk to Ellen again. Or Joy Ann. Or Marcie."

"Let's start with Marcie. I get the impression Buddy didn't really tell Ellen anything. And Joy Ann was concerned enough about his disappearance to call the sheriff's department twice about it. If she knew Buddy was involved in something that might have gotten him killed, I think she would have told the police last year."

"Okay. I'll see if I can con Marcie into meeting us for a cup of coffee this afternoon if you can get away, that is."

I glanced at Mom and waited for her nod of approval before telling Lottie I could go. I'd spent a lot of time this week away from the campground and I was beginning to feel a little guilty about it.

"Who else is a possible suspect?" Mom asked. "Even if Buddy and Mike were running a theft scheme, he might have been killed by someone else over a completely different matter."

"Well, a couple of years ago Andy Treeling and Buddy came to blows over a hunting site," Lottie volunteered.

"What?" I turned to her, shocked to hear that about friendly, easygoing Andy Treeling.

Lottie nodded. "Andy had the hunting rights for the Besemer property on a handshake deal and had been going there for five years, when all of a sudden Buddy shows up saying he got permission from Floyd Besemer to hunt there exclusively and that Andy had to get out."

Mom sucked in a breath. "Ooo, you don't mess with someone's hunting property."

"No you don't," Lottie agreed. "And it wasn't nice of Buddy to go behind Andy's back like that and make a deal with Floyd. Also wasn't nice for Floyd to grant Buddy the hunting rights without telling Andy, but Floyd isn't one who likes to tell people bad news. They both worked each other over pretty bad, and Andy absolutely hated Buddy after that."

I snatched the pad and pen from Lottie and wrote down Andy's name. I couldn't imagine him as a killer, but if we were going to list Mike as a possible suspect, then we pretty much had to put Andy down as well.

"Are there any other people who got into fights with Buddy?" Mom asked. "Anyone who threatened him?"

Lottie snorted. "Oh, plenty of people threatened him. Back when Marcie's husband was alive Buddy worked for him. It wasn't very long before Jason found out that Buddy was using his tools and equipment for his own side jobs.

Jason fired Buddy, and the two were frosty with each other ever since.

"But Jason can't be the murderer, since he died years ago," I pointed out. "And I doubt if Marcie was part of the feud since she was named as one of Buddy's lovers."

"True, although it is odd that the body we're assuming is Buddy's was found in the woods next to property owned by Marcie," Mom commented.

"Or that could just be a coincidence. Like I said, the field isn't being farmed, and it's down a rarely used road. The location could have just been chosen because it was convenient and private."

I wrote Marcie's name down on the pad next to Mike's and Andy's, even though I couldn't think of a reasonable motive for her to kill Buddy. Maybe one would come to light when we spoke to her.

"Was there anything in those two boxes you took that might be a clue?" I asked.

Lottie held up her hands. "I've been through both boxes of papers and there wasn't anything in there that stood out—other than the fact that Buddy was probably cheating on his taxes. He had copies of his returns going back for the last six years. I'm no accountant, but according to them, Buddy should have been on food stamps and public housing."

"So it looks like we've got Mike, Andy or Marcie," Mom said, reading the names off the notepad.

One of them might be Buddy's killer. And if I were a betting woman, I'd be putting my money on Mike Allen.

CHAPTER 18

*L*ater that afternoon I went back to the house to shower and change in preparation for Lottie's and my visit with Marcie Boarding. I'd just collected Elvis and tied him behind the counter to relax with Mom when I saw Lottie's car once more pulling into the parking area. I climbed in and she drove into Reckless.

With a feeling of déjà vu, Lottie parked and we walked toward The Coffee Dog. This time instead of Tony Marconi, a woman sat at one of the café tables out front. Marcie Boarding was wearing tan linen pants and a silky white button-down shirt, accessorized with a thick gold chain. Small gold hoops decorated her ears. Her snow-white hair was pulled back into a messy bun with a few loose strands framing her face. By her side sat Sarge, the Doberman looking as much an accessory as the jewelry she wore.

We greeted each other, and Lottie ran in to get everyone's coffee orders while I sat next to Marcie, Sarge a silent buffer between us. The dog shot me a quick, judgmental glance before returning to his horizon-focused stare.

"Are you excited for the next tracking event?" I asked, selecting a small-talk topic until Lottie returned.

Marcie wrinkled her nose. "We'll probably skip it. Sarge doesn't like tracking people. He does better with scent detection."

I kept my mouth shut about Sarge's poor performance in last week's scent detection event. Elvis had done even worse, and people in glass houses…

"Everyone is saying that body Elvis found in the woods is Buddy Hooper." I glanced at the door of the coffee shop, feeling guilty about jumping into our investigation without Lottie. I never was all that good at small talk, and I got the impression Marcie wasn't interested in discussing the lack of rain this summer or the performance of local sports teams.

"I figured they'd find his body eventually," Marcie replied.

I stared at her open-mouthed. Was she confessing to murder? Had she known the body was there?

"We were an item, you know," Marcie shot me a knowing glance. "I'm sure everyone has told you. Jason is probably turning over in his grave. He hated Buddy. Mainly because he knew I was having an affair with him."

Wait. What? "You were sleeping with Buddy when Jason was still alive?"

She nodded, as if that were a perfectly acceptable thing to do. "Buddy and I started our fling about a month after he moved to town. I cared for my husband, but we hadn't been intimate in years. What Buddy and I had was just sex—well, as much as it can be just sex when you're having a long-term affair with someone."

"And after Jason died…?" I asked.

Marcie shrugged. "We just kept on with things, only we weren't as cautious about keeping it quiet. With Jason gone, I really didn't care who in the town knew. What I did in my bedroom was my own business."

I didn't agree with her having an affair when she was married, but I *did* agree with that last statement.

Lottie came out the door of the coffee shop, holding a carrier with three coffees in it. "What did I miss?" she asked as she distributed our drinks.

I looked back and forth between Lottie and Marcie, uncertain how to sum up our conversation so far.

"I'd been screwing Buddy Hooper pretty much since he arrived in Reckless." Marcie took a quick sip of her coffee. "Jason knew, but I kept it quiet and discrete until he died. I never wanted anything more from Buddy than sex, and he felt the same."

Now Lottie was the one with the open mouth. She sat heavily into her chair and glanced at me wide-eyed.

"Do you have any idea what might have happened to him?" I asked

"I assume he pissed the wrong person off." Marcie's voice was brittle. "Buddy had a habit of that. Maybe he screwed the wrong woman, or cheated the wrong guy." She gave us each a sad smile. "I know you're wondering why I didn't report him missing. I didn't feel it was my place. Buddy made his own decisions and lived his own life. Either one of us could bail on our fling at any time with no need to explain. There was a chance he'd left town and didn't let me know, but I had a feeling something was wrong. I just...knew."

I absolutely didn't understand this relationship of theirs, but I wasn't going to judge—at least not now. I'd probably do plenty of judging when I was home and telling this story to Mom.

"Joy Ann said he had some big business deal and was planning on leaving town soon," Lottie said.

Marcie shrugged. "It's a possibility he was planning to leave, but Buddy always said that sort of thing. It was his setup to ditching a lover if things were getting too serious.

He'd been here ten years. I had no reason to believe he was leaving anytime soon, but then again, we didn't exactly talk about that sort of stuff."

"I heard you wanted Buddy to be exclusive with you," I said, thinking of Joy Ann's comment.

She laughed. "I didn't want to end up with any STDs, that's for sure. We used protection, but would I have preferred if Buddy wasn't screwing other women? Yes. Ultimately, that wasn't my call to make. He did what he wanted. I did what I wanted. And if either of us decided we didn't like that, well, we were free to leave."

"Did you ever loan him money?" Lottie asked. "I heard he had a lot of financial problems."

"Nope. Money changes things. It makes a relationship... transactional. I might have committed adultery, but there are some lines I won't cross."

I was getting the impression that Marcie Boarding was not our murderer. She was completely capable of it—I had no doubt there—but I couldn't see a motive. She was happy with the casual booty calls, and from what she and the other women had said, Buddy never seemed to want more from his partners either. There was no reason for her to kill the man.

She may not have had a hand in his murder, but she might have been involved in the theft ring—or at least know something about it. And as weirdly fascinating as this relationship talk was, I wanted to get us back to the investigation.

"The GPS collars that everyone in the club uses, I heard you bought them through Mike Allen? At a ten percent discount?" I asked.

Marcie blinked at the topic change, then sniffed. "Mike Allen is as much of a scammer as Buddy was, he just hides it under an expensive suit where Buddy kept it all out front. Yes, he sold us the collars at a ten percent discount. He's president of the club, so there was some pressure for everyone to buy one. I'm pretty sure he got them either for free or at cost and pocketed the difference. The man is a total weasel."

"Did Buddy buy a collar?" I thought about the GPS collar in the box of paperwork. Buddy didn't seem the sort to be pressured into anything, and that collar was far more expensive than the models I'd seen the Reckless Sniffer Club dogs sporting.

Marcie laughed. "No. He told Mike to shove off. Buddy had already sold Daisy by that point and wasn't about to spend a bunch of money on something he couldn't use. Buddy quit the club soon after that."

"Because of the fight with Mike?" Lottie asked.

"No, because he didn't have a dog and decided not to get another one after selling Daisy." Marcie sipped her coffee. "He was taking on some additional hauling jobs, and didn't have the time for a dog."

There was something about the way she'd broken her gaze and looked at her coffee cup that made me think there was a lot she wasn't telling us.

"Buddy had a lot of new and unopened electronics," I said. "A gaming computer. A laptop. Several cell phones. There was a fifteen-hundred-dollar GPS tracking collar in a box with his bank statements. Joy Ann said he gave her a brand-new cell phone before the model was even available in stores."

Marcie's mouth twisted into a wry smile. "Really? I paid for mine. That little tart got hers for free?"

Oops.

"Buddy sold me some new electronics at a really great price," Marcie admitted. "My phone. A laptop. One of those home security camera systems. I didn't ask where he'd gotten it all and I didn't want to know. He was a hay farmer who occasionally hauled heavy equipment, so I was pretty sure these all fell out of the back of a truck, if you know what I mean."

I did know what she meant, thanks to Mom and Lottie.

"A few weeks after I bought the cell phone I was at a club meeting and Mike saw me use it." She smirked. "It wasn't even available in stores yet. He ran over, demanding to know where I got it. I refused to tell him, of course, because it was none of his business. He asked me if I'd gotten it from Buddy, and I just told him that I had connections."

"Mike's a VP of Purchasing for Rio Grande," Lottie mused. "He'd know what the latest devices were and when they were supposed to go on sale."

But why would Mike care that Marcie managed to get a phone pre-release? He shouldn't care unless he suspected that phone might tie him to a crime.

"I'm not a dumb woman," Marcie informed us. "At first I figured that Mike was getting demo stuff and selling it to Buddy who was flipping it, and Mike was worried it would get traced back to him since demo stuff isn't supposed to be resold. But then I remembered Mike selling us the collars with only a ten percent discount, and I knew there was no way he'd sell Buddy demo equipment with enough of a discount to make it worthwhile for Buddy to resell. That's when I figured it must have been stolen. Mike was involved somehow in the theft, and Buddy had been reselling part of his 'payment' or had kept a few items he wasn't supposed to keep."

"And when Buddy went missing, you didn't think it might have something to do with these stolen electronics?" Lottie's voice was high pitched with incredulity. "You didn't suspect that someone in the theft ring might have murdered Buddy? That Mike might be angry enough at Buddy exposing their crimes to kill him?"

Marcie's eyebrows rose. "I figured it was just small-time theft and nothing that would get someone killed. Besides, the only things I had that might implicate Buddy in a theft was a laptop and a cell phone. That was it. There was nothing tying Mike into any of this, and I honestly wasn't sure if Mike was involved or not. He may have just been aware of a theft ring at his company, and suspected Buddy of being involved."

"You know, Mike Allen was bidding on Buddy's storage unit when it was up for auction," I told Marcie. "Ellen Preston won the bid, and she said Mike bought the electronics off of her," Lottie said to Marcie.

"Did he?" The other woman frowned. "It *does* sound like Mike was involved in some sort of theft scam with Buddy. Maybe Mike did kill him. Or maybe there was another partner who killed him. Greed and fear does horrible things to a person."

Yes, it did.

"Well, I'm sure the police will get to the bottom of this." Lottie downed the rest of her coffee. "It was so good to catch up with you Marcie. Sassy and I really need to get going. Thanks for meeting us."

"It was good to catch up. And thank you for the coffee." Marcie put a hand on Sarge's head and the dog broke his thousand-yard stare to look up at her with adoring eyes.

Lottie and I walked back to the car in silence. Once we were inside and on the road, Lottie turned to me.

"I'm glad I never got on that woman's bad side. She's cold. Icy. Terrifying."

"She is," I agreed. And as I watched the scenery go by, I wondered what Marcie Boarding was really capable of. She hadn't been bothered about buying stolen electronics. She hadn't been bothered enough about Buddy's disappearance and supposed death to even go to the police. She'd done nothing even though she suspected Mike might be involved somehow.

Buddy hadn't mattered that much to her. I wondered if her husband, Jason meant that much to her either. Honestly, the only person I thought Marcie Boarding cared about wasn't a person at all, but her Doberman, Sarge.

CHAPTER 19

*T*hursday morning was chaos as usual. Guests were checking out, and I was a ball of anxiety since this week none of the cabin guests had left early. I'd somehow need to clean a dozen cabins between noon and four before the new guests began arriving. Actually I'd have less than four hours, since some of the cabin guests might be a little tardy getting out, and we often had new campers arrive early. Ideally I'd like to have all the cabins ready to go at two.

Once more I thought about Nikki at the Chat-n-Chew and decided that in addition to helping cover the store during our cruises, I could also offer her some hours helping clean the cabins for guest turnover.

Mom came in early at nine to help out, and Austin arrived at about the same time to get a head start on trash and general clean up in preparation for new guests. If he finished early, I was absolutely going to press him into the service of cabin-cleaning and laundry duty.

One person who hadn't shown up as expected this morning was Jake. Again. It was the second morning that I hadn't seen his truck pull in. His boat still remained docked at the slip. I'd texted him a summary of Lottie's and my meeting with Marcie yesterday but hadn't heard back. Maybe he'd gotten a lead on the case. Maybe those dental records of Buddy's had come in.

Maybe he was just busy.

Putting it out of my mind, I went out on the porch of the camp store to sweep and water the hanging baskets of flowers before the sun and heat wilted them. I was just finishing the last bunch of begonias when Allie and Ellie came over to say goodbye to me, and more importantly, to Elvis. Their father had checked out earlier, and the girls said they were almost done breaking down their campsite. It was a tearful farewell, and Elvis got lots of hugs and a handful of biscuits. I was sad to see the girls go, and hoped they and their father would be back again soon.

The girls had just left when a familiar BMW sedan came up the drive, going a good bit faster than the ten-mile-per-hour speed limit I'd posted. Normally I'd scold the driver, but I was sure Lottie had a good reason for speeding. Abandoning my watering can, I ran down the steps and jogged over to meet her as she pulled the car around the loop in front of the store.

"What happened?" I shouted, all sorts of emergencies about her children or Scotty running through my head.

"Get in," Lottie shouted back. "They're getting ready to pull the truck out and I want to be there. Half the town is there. Hurry."

By that point Mom had come out of the store and towards us to see what all the commotion was about. I pivoted between her and Lottie and held up my hands.

"What truck? What are you talking about? It's Thursday, Lottie. I can't leave. It's check-out, and check-in day."

"Buddy's truck. At least, everyone believes it's Buddy's truck. I should have known that would be the perfect place to dump it, although it's a shame to ruin a nice truck like that. I guess ruining a nice truck is better than going to jail for murder, though."

It was starting to make sense. I still had no idea where Buddy's truck had been found or exactly what was going on, but I was just as excited as Lottie that someone may have found a vital piece of evidence in the man's disappearance.

Although, that still didn't change the fact that it was Thursday, and I couldn't go running off when it was our busiest day of the week.

"Go." Mom urged, taking Elvis's leash from me. "I'll take care of things here."

"I've got to clean all those cabins and prep them for new guests," I protested. "Even with Austin helping, I'm going to be scrambling to get it done in time."

"You can't even start cleaning them until the guests leave at noon," Mom countered. "That gives you over two hours before you need to be back."

"And I'll help you," Lottie promised. "With the two of us and Austin all cleaning and washing the sheets, we'll be done in record time. We'll be back by noon, I promise."

"Okay." I really did want to see if this was Buddy's truck, and I wasn't about to pass on the offer of help, either.

I shouted a hasty thanks to Mom, then got in Lottie's car. She took a little more care with her speed exiting the campground, but then gunned it once we hit the road.

"Where exactly did they find this truck?" I asked as I made sure my seatbelt was secure.

"In the lake! Remember Tony said some guys had to check out the waterfront of his development before he backfilled everything for the beach area? The divers found a truck about thirty feet from the shore."

"Where the cliff originally was, right?" I asked. "The one

you all used to dive off of when you were kids? The one with the rope swing or tire swing?"

"That one." Lottie bounced a little with excitement. "The water is really deep there because of the cliff and the drop off."

"So you think someone killed Buddy then drove his truck off the cliff before Tony bulldozed it all?" I frowned. "Weren't there towns down there before the valley was flooded to make the lake? Maybe this truck was abandoned and has been down there since the lake was formed."

"The divers said it's a newer model truck," Lottie said. "And although it had a good coating of silt on it, it wasn't buried like you would expect a truck to be if it had sat down there for a hundred years."

"Could it be someone else's truck?" I asked. "As horrible as it sounds, maybe someone drove over the cliff to commit suicide. Or maybe someone ditched the truck before it was repossessed, sort of a screw-you to the finance company?"

"Maybe, but from what the divers described, it sounds a lot like Buddy's truck," Lottie said. "The license plates had been taken off, but I'm pretty sure once the sheriff's department gets it out of the lake and checks the VIN number, it'll come back that it's Buddy's truck."

In record time we were pulling into the Swallows Landing Development, past the condos and townhomes that I'd recently seen from pictures on Tony's phone. We weren't the only ones here to watch the "Raising Of The Truck". Vehicles were parked all along the streets next to nearly-finished homes, and crowds were gathered on a level dirt strip that would soon be covered with sand. Lottie parked sideways half in the dirt. She had the car off and was out of the driver's seat in record time. I climbed out as well, and had to jog to keep up with her speed-walk.

Crowds were gathered around the water's edge, giving a

large crane a respectful distance. Chains extended from the top of the crane down into the water. I recognized Deputy Sean Cork in uniform talking to a man wearing a hard hat who was, I presumed, talking to the crane operator through a walkie-talkie. I also recognized Jake, and Tony.

Tony glanced over and made his way toward us as Lottie and I squeezed through the crowd to get a better look at what was going on in the water.

"Oh good. They haven't brought it up yet," Lottie said. "I was worried we'd miss the big reveal."

Tony stood next to her, looking far less excited. "I was hoping this could all be kept quiet, but it looks like half the town is here."

Lottie snorted. "A truck found in the lake? Possibly to cover up a crime? You bet half the town is going to come out for this one."

"I didn't expect this at all when the divers came out the other day. It was supposed to be a routine dive to document anything historic on the lake bed before I dumped in the sand." Tony shook his head. "The divers said they didn't even need the metal detector to see the truck down there. They said it looked like had probably only been in the lake for a year, give or take a few months. License plates were missing, but they said it wasn't just some old truck that someone was junking into the lake. Said it looked like it wasn't more than five or six years old. Nice heavy-duty work truck. F350 or something. Those are worth something even in scrap, so I doubt the owner intentionally put it into the lake."

"Drunk driving?" a woman next to us guessed. "I remember that drop off was steep, but I didn't think a vehicle would be able to make it to the edge of that cliff."

"We'd cleared most of the brush and rocks away by April of last year," Tony told her. "Before I had it all leveled, we'd barricaded the area so someone wouldn't accidently go over the edge. Whoever drove off the cliff would have needed to move barricades. I can't see a drunk driver doing that. And if it was a suicide, then whoever drove over the cliff wouldn't have been alive to put the barricades back when they were done. We were really careful about safety, and I would have gotten a report if someone had showed up one morning to find them moved."

"When did you all level that cliff out?" I asked Tony.

"End of June and that first week in July. I remember because I was really hoping they could get it done before the holiday." He turned toward me. "That means the truck went into the lake mid-June or earlier."

Which was right around the time Buddy went missing.

"I wonder if there's a body in the truck," the woman next to us said rather gleefully. "Someone disposed of a body and the truck at the same time. Just like in those mob movies."

I stared at her, appalled.

"There better not be a body in the truck," Tony said, making the sign of the cross on his chest. "If there is, no one is going to buy those single family homes. "People will break their contracts. Values in the condos and townhomes will plummet. Everyone will claim the ghost of the victim is haunting the development. I'll never be able to sell another house again."

And now I stared at Tony, equally appalled at the man's priorities.

"There won't be a dead body because it's Buddy Hooper's truck, and I'm positive it was his body that was found in the woods Saturday," Lottie announced confidently. "It's got to be Buddy's truck down there. He drove an F350, late model and the timeline fits. He went missing in early June, and this truck went over the cliff right around then. Buddy vanished. His truck vanished. His tractor vanished."

Tony paled.

"Was it blue?" the woman next to us asked. "Buddy drove a dark blue truck. Although down at the bottom of the lake, it might have looked black."

Two figures in dive suits surfaced near the chains and we fell silent, our attention on them. One gave a thumb's-up, and the pair made their way to the shore. Once they were safely out of the way, the man talking to Sean said something into his walkie-talkie, and the crane started lifting. I wasn't sure how deep the water was at that point, but the chains coming out of the water seemed to go on forever before the dark hood of the truck broke free from the lake.

"Looks navy blue to me," the woman next to us commented.

It did look navy blue on the parts where the water had washed off the silt. Dirt covered the wheels and the glass, but the paint was still shiny on the sections where it was visible. Once the truck was clear of the water, the crane operator held it in place a few moments, letting the water drain from the cab and the bed. Then he slowly spun the crane around and lowered the truck carefully onto the dirt beach.

Everyone watching pivoted as well, staring at the truck with wide eyes and expectant expressions.

"No body, no body, no body," Tony chanted under his breath.

Sean approached the truck, donning gloves and wrenching the driver's door open. More water poured out. The deputy waited for it to subside before lifting himself up to read off the VIN number from the metal plate on the dash.

"That's a match," he called out to Jake who was writing the number down on a pad of paper.

I could see even from this distance that the sometimes deputy looked exhausted. It made me feel guilty for my paranoid thoughts about his absence and non-response to my text. The poor guy had probably been working non-stop for the last two days.

Jake walked over toward us while Steff and her crew moved in to begin processing the truck and any contents that might have survived a year in the lake.

"We'll need you to come to the station with Sean and I to answer some questions," Jake said to Tony.

Tony paled. "I didn't kill him. I had no reason to kill Buddy. Yeah, the guy left me hanging with months of lost rent, plus what I had to pay to get rid of all his stuff and clean the farmhouse, but that's not reason to kill someone. Either way, I'd have to be an idiot to dump his truck in the lake at one of my developments. And even more of an idiot to give the green light to people diving down there before I filled it in."

"True," Lottie chimed in. "If you killed Buddy and drove his truck over that cliff you would have just gone ahead and filled in that section of the lake without bothering with any permits. Better to ask forgiveness than permission if you're a murderer trying to cover up a crime."

"I'm not sure that's super helpful," I told Lottie.

"Also, Buddy disappeared before the eviction was finalized," Lottie continued. "And his truck would have needed to go over the cliff before the eviction was finalized. Why would Tony kill Buddy in early June when he still had hopes of getting his back rent?"

"The truck was found in the lake at your development," Jake said to Tony. "We need to have an official statement regarding when that cliff was graded down as well as any security measures you had at the time. Plus we need to talk to you about what was left at the farmhouse during the eviction."

Tony sucked in a breath. "Sean was with me. He served the eviction papers. He saw that there was no one in the house, and that only some old furniture and junk was left behind."

"Sean didn't go into the barn," Jake pointed out.

"There was just hay in the barn," Tony shot back. "I sold it. Maybe I shouldn't have, but I did. Is that a crime?"

"Just hay?" Jake fixed Tony with one of those cop-stares that always put a knot in my stomach and made me feel like I was on the edge of being arrested for something myself.

Tony hesitated, shifting his weight as Jake didn't speak.

"The tractor," he finally admitted. "The tractor was in there with the hay. I sold it to Dean Hellerman. I didn't say anything about it because I wasn't sure if the eviction meant that the tractor was considered abandoned or not. The guy owed me back rent, plus my time and court fees, plus having to hire people to clean out the house and haul stuff to the dump. I figured he owed me, and if he took off and left the tractor behind, it was mine to keep."

I frowned at Tony, my opinion of him seriously tarnished.

"I didn't kill him," Tony insisted. "I swear the last time I saw Buddy Hooper was the last week in May when I put the eviction notice on his door. He was driving out with a load of hay just as I was pulling in. He didn't show up at the final hearing on June fifteenth, and he wasn't there when the deputy and I did the final eviction."

"I never said anything about you killing Buddy Hooper," Jake said. "But I do need you to come down to the station and answer some questions about the development and about the tractor. We're not arresting you. We're not even making you ride down in Sean's squad car."

Tony eyed him, then nodded and headed for his car.

"I got your message, Sassy." Jake scrubbed a hand over his face. "I'll be by in an hour or two to pick up those boxes from you and Lottie."

"We'll be cleaning the cabins, but we'll swing by Lottie's

house on the way back and get the ones she has. I'll take all the boxes over to the camp store and you can pick them up from Mom." I eyed him. "Is it Mike Allen? Is he the murderer?"

"It's an active investigation." Jake waved a finger at me, and then at Lottie. "You two be careful. I'm grateful you all dug around into Buddy's disappearance, but this is now a murder case. That means there's a murderer out there who has killed once and probably won't hesitate to do it again."

I shivered.

"Did Stef identify the body yet?" Lottie asked him, not as bothered by the warning as I was.

"The dental records matched. It's Buddy Hooper." Jake turned around and headed for his truck.

Lottie and I stayed for a while as did most of the crowd, but watching Steff and her crew take pictures and process the truck wasn't as thrilling as the television shows would have us believe. Slowly the crowd dwindled, and at eleven thirty we left as well.

It somehow felt anticlimactic. The body Elvis had found was Buddy's. Buddy's truck had been found, and we now knew what had happened to his tractor. And hopefully the police were closing in on the killer.

Everything was coming together, and Lottie and I should be happy to hand over what we'd learned and let the authorities handle things from here.

But was there enough evidence to put Buddy's murderer behind bars? Or would the killer get away with the crime?

CHAPTER 20

*W*e were efficient cleaning machines. Lottie and I scrubbed floors, dusted, and changed sheets while Austin did the laundry and took care of cleaning the buildings housing the bathrooms and the other common areas. Once more I thought about how I could make these cabins attractive to winter guests. It wasn't only the heating systems and weatherproofing that were on my mind, but the fact that none of these cabins had plumbing. Winter guests would need to tromp through the cold and snow to get to the bathroom building. That building had a really effective heater, but it still wouldn't be pleasant to deal with the cold in between the cabins and the facilities.

There was no way plumbing and bathroom extensions could happen this year, or probably even next year. The cost would most likely require me to get a loan, and I'd need enough proof that the campground was on solid financial footing before I could borrow any more against it. I'd just shelled out an unexpected amount for a boat motor. That was my big expense for the year.

"I'm worried about Tony," Lottie spoke up, interrupting

my thoughts. "I know Jake assured him he wasn't being arrested, but doesn't it look bad that Buddy's truck was found in the lake at his development?"

"I think it was pretty clear that he didn't know the truck was there," I assured her. "Yes, he did kinda have motive. If he knew that he was never getting the money out of Buddy, then killing him so he could get the tractor, the hay, and whatever else was in that barn out of the eviction process would be a way to come out even financially—or ahead, actually."

"But Tony's rich," Lottie protested. "His family had money, and with his business savvy he's really grown the company since he took over. He's absolutely the type who watches the bottom line, but that back rent couldn't have been more than a blip on his balance statement. He'd fret over the loss, but then he'd write it off and move on. He wouldn't murder someone and risk his businesses and jail time just for some back rent."

"I know you and Tony have a long history, growing up together in Reckless, but I think he's a bit opportunistic when it comes to his business dealings," I said cautiously. I didn't want to offend Lottie or criticize her friend too harshly, but Tony was beginning to strike me as a little underhanded.

She shrugged. "That's what it's like in business. Scotty has to cross the line with his sales job as well. Sometimes that's what you have to do in the industry to be competitive."

I didn't like that one bit. I'd been in the corporate world, and had seen people try to justify unethical behavior under the banner of being competitive, or the excuse of "everyone does it," or the other excuse of needing to meet shareholder expectations on profits. It never sat well with me, and I'd always been ready to risk losing my job rather than cross that line. Lottie was my best friend, and I knew she was a kind and caring person. If she found herself in that situation, I had no doubt that she'd make the right decision, but it worried me that she was ready to excuse unethical or borderline illegal behavior in others.

"How did Jake even find out about the tractor?" Lottie said as she started cleaning the windows. "It happened almost a year ago. What caused Jake to look into it now after all that time? How did he even make the connection between Dean Hellerman's purchase from Tony and Buddy?"

I squirmed a bit, feeling guilt that I absolutely should not be feeling. "When Jake and I were at the Chat-n-Chew Tuesday night, I told him that Buddy had paid off his truck and his tractor, and that he had thirty grand in his checking account according to the last statement. He got a funny look on his face, so I'm guessing he knew that Dean Hellerman bought a tractor from Tony, did the math as far as the time-line went, then connected the dots."

Lottie nodded. "That makes sense. Jake's got that farmette up on the mountain with horses and a bit of land. It's reasonable that he would have heard about a tractor being sold. Tony wouldn't be a man you'd expect to be selling a used tractor. He's a developer and he lives in some big six-thou-sand-square-foot house on the lake. The house takes up about ninety percent of his lot. He doesn't even need a riding mower, let alone a tractor."

Lottie knew an awful lot about Tony, and that kind of worried me. Yes, Lottie was a gossip and was very knowl-edgeable about the goings-on in Reckless and in the county, but she seemed overly aware about Tony's life. Everything I'd seen about Lottie pointed to her being a devoted wife and mother, but I believed there were cracks in the foundation of her marriage—whether she admitted it or not. And Tony was a terrible flirt who'd admitted to me that he'd had a child-hood crush on Lottie. Would he be a temptation my friend couldn't resist? I didn't really know Scotty. I wasn't a big fan of his based on what little I did know. But whether I thought Lottie's husband was a jerk or not was irrelevant. She was married, and I knew how seriously she took her marriage vows. She might be tempted into an affair with an attractive man she'd grown up with and who clearly was attracted to her, but an affair would crush Lottie. She'd feel guilty. She'd feel that she betrayed her vows, her beliefs, her husband, and her children. I didn't want her to go there. I didn't want her to make a decision she'd regret later.

"Do you think what he did was illegal?" Lottie asked. "Tony I mean. With the tractor. And the hay. And I'm sure there were other farm implements in that barn he sold as well, like Buddy's hay wagon. Was that wrong?"

I took a deep breath and slowly let it out, trying to think of a good way to phrase my response. "I don't like what Tony did. The man has money. He's not struggling to pay his mortgage or put food on the table for his kids. I don't think it was illegal of him to sell what is probably considered under the law as abandoned property in an eviction, but I don't think it was ethical. He had to have known that a man who was being evicted for non-payment of rent, who was supposedly in over his head in debt, wouldn't abandon a tractor, hay, and other farm tools. Tony easily sold that tractor. He had to have known that Buddy would have either done the same, or skipped town with the tractor so he could use it in a future job."

Lottie nodded. "Honestly I don't think Tony considered all that. He's not a bad guy. I doubt he thought something horrible had happened to Buddy. He just knew the guy stiffed him, and probably felt lucky that he could recover the debt with what was left behind."

I made a noncommittal noise and tucked the sheets in under the mattress, thinking that I'd just have to let this one rest. It would be one of those things Lottie and I had differing opinions on.

"I don't know how they'll ever prove who drove that truck over the cliff, unless there's some evidence in the vehicle that survived being in the lake for almost a year," Lottie said after a few moments of silence. "Any security footage is probably long gone. The barriers were removed when Tony had it all graded, so any fingerprints would be smudged over by this point. There weren't any occupied houses then for residents to have noticed someone driving the truck in under the cover of darkness."

"Mmm," I agreed, thinking that the killer probably did drive the truck over the cliff in the middle of the night. During the day there would be workers there to have seen it all happen. "Wouldn't the entire construction site have been fenced off during that time?" I wondered. "It seems they would need to do that for insurance liability, so curious kids didn't come by and get hurt, and so someone didn't pull up in the middle of the night and drive off with a truckload of lumber or copper piping."

"That's a good point," Lottie said. "And just like a worker would have said something if they'd come in and found the barriers to the cliff removed, I'm sure someone would have said something if the locks had been cut or the fencing damaged, or the gate wide open."

"So either one of Tony's employees let someone in, or the killer had the key or code to get in themselves," I pointed out. "And how would he have gotten home? I'm assuming the murderer drove the truck there, but after he drove it off the cliff, what happened? Did he walk home? Have someone give him a ride? Was there a second person involved?"

"I can't see the murderer involving a second person in a coverup and opening himself up to blackmail," Lottie pointed out.

"So he walked," I decided. If it was too risky to involve a second person, then it was probably too risky to call for an Uber pickup at a construction site in the middle of the night.

"Either the killer lived within a few miles of the development, or he's a runner. Or a cyclist who put his bike in the back of Buddy's truck before ditching it."

"Wouldn't someone have noticed a person jogging or biking down the road after dark?" I frowned, thinking that the road leading into the development was fairly well-traveled.

"Maybe someone did and they'll come forward now that they know the significance of what they saw," Lottie said. "Maybe the killer is a local who convinced a construction employee to give him a key so he could have 'one last dive' in the lake off the cliff for nostalgia's sake before it was bull-dozed down. Once that employee hears about the truck, he'll remember that night and come forward. Someone had to have seen something—whether it was a person dragging a large heavy tarp through that field into the woods, or someone on the road late at night, or someone being let in to the development one night last June. *Someone* saw something."

Lottie was right. And hopefully that someone would connect the dots and realize they'd seen a murderer.

We were done cleaning the cabins by two-thirty. Lottie went home, and Austin insisted on finishing up the laundry, saying that the small amount of RV and tent site cleanup he needed to do wouldn't take long. I took a very refreshing shower and was back at the camp store at three, feeling less sweaty and ready for our new guests. Mom told me that Jake had already picked up the boxes and dropped off the thermos I'd loaned him. I only had a few seconds to regret that I hadn't been able to grill him about the case before our check-in rush started.

I gave Mom the thumbs-up on any cabin rentals, then took my place beside her behind the counter, announcing that anyone who had reserved a tent or a camper site could shift over into my lane. We worked straight through until five o'clock when I told Mom to call it quits for the evening. With a break in between customers, I took Elvis for a quick walk around the camp store so he could pee and stretch his legs. We ended our walk at the lakefront where we walked down the dock to look at the boats.

The sight of my pontoon boat in the water made me giddy with excitement. I already had activities planned for Friday night, but this weekend I intended on making up some flyers for the sunset cruises. We'd do our test-voyage Saturday night, and if all went well, I'd planned for our first official cruise Monday night.

Excited to get my pontoon boat earning money, I texted Flora, asking if she could watch the camp store for a few hours Saturday evening while we did our test run. Once I received her confirmation, I sent more texts out to Lottie, Danielle, Sierra, and Jake with the date and time for the sunset cruise. With me, Austin, and Mom, there would be seven of us. Back at the camp store, I made a list of foods and supplies I'd need and started work on the flyers to hand out to campers.

Filled with plans for the cruises and busy with our new guests, I didn't think about the murder again until the next morning when I started going over everything again in my mind. I pulled out my notepad and looked through all I'd written, from Lottie's and my meeting with Tony to our meeting with Marcie. The truck had been found. The tractor had been found. But there was one item on my to-do list that I'd forgotten about: the trailer.

CHAPTER 21

*R*eckless Neighbors App:
Want to watch the sunset over the lake while sipping champagne on a pontoon boat? Want to cruise the waters and hear about the history of Savage Lake, or the ghosts that haunt the area? Call or e-mail Reckless Camper Campground and reserve your spot now!

Once Mom arrived at the camp store at ten o'clock, I headed back to the house and began assembling the materials for our wine cork arts-and-crafts projects. There would be cookies and brownies courtesy of The Coffee Dog, and plenty of fun projects for kids and adults. I'd gathered up dozens of felt squares from a bin in the attic and used paint markers to create tic-tac-toe boards. Children (or adults) would decorate corks as squirrels and blue jays for the opposing pieces. Adults could make wreaths or trivets with their corks and paint them however they chose. The beer cap art had been such a hit that I'd asked local places to save their wine corks for me as well. Bonfire. Sweet snacks. BYOB. Crafts. It should be a wonderful Friday evening and a great way to kick off our new guests' vacations.

Lottie pulled in at noon to pick me up. I let Mom know I was leaving, gave Elvis a pat, and climbed into the BMW. It was a thirty minute drive into Derwood to Big Rig Rentals. On the way we discussed the case, went over all the evidence, then conversation switched to the trial run of my sunset cruise tomorrow night.

"What should I wear?" Lottie asked, practically bouncing in excitement.

"Something comfortable. Rubber soled shoes. Maybe a sweater in case it gets chilly." I thought about it a second. "You won't need a purse or anything, but maybe bring your cell phone for pictures."

"Champagne and charcuterie." Lottie grinned. "Do you want me to bring some muffins? Or a seven bean dip?"

I couldn't imagine trying to eat a seven bean dip on a boat, and the muffins and chips were liable to be crumbled up all over the deck by the end of the evening.

"No—thank you, though. I want Saturday night to be exactly as it's going to be when I take guests out, so it will be a true trial run."

We debated brie versus goat cheese and salami versus chorizo until we pulled into the parking lot of the rental place.

Big Rig Rentals was fenced in with a gate that had a security access pad. Outside of the enclosure was a huge parking area and a small building that I took to be the office. Inside the enclosure were rows upon rows of box and flatbed trailers, construction equipment, cement mixers, and something that looked like an asphalt spreader. I followed Lottie inside, where she greeted the man behind the counter by name. Of course.

"Hi Stanley. How's Brenda doing?"

Stanley looked to be in seventies with a faced tanned into the texture of leather. Round framed glasses enlarged his brown eyes and wisps of short silver hair surrounded a bald dome.

The man smiled, revealing snow-white teeth. "Lottie! It's good to see you, girl. Brenda's doing well. She's off with her friends painting a bunch of cows." Stanley turned to me. "My wife does plein air painting. There's so many landscapes, bridges, and livestock hanging on my walls that you can barely see the color of the paint. She keeps it up, we might need to buy a bigger house."

I smiled, thinking that I should invite Brenda's plein air group to the campground. I could sell small art kits, and guests could join in if they liked.

"How's the wedding planning?" Stanley asked Lottie.

Lottie shrugged. "It's a struggle. Amanda keeps changing her mind. But I'm excited that she's going to have it in Reckless rather than Atlanta as she originally planned."

"It'll be good to see her again." Stanley rubbed his hands together and straightened his glasses. "So what can I do for you ladies?"

"My friend Sassy and I are doing some amateur sleuthing on Buddy Hooper's disappearance," Lottie told him. "We were hoping you could give us some details on a trailer he rented June of last year. Probably early morning June eleventh."

Stanley headed over to a wall of filing cabinets. "I heard that body that was found in the woods last Saturday was his. Buddy was a shiftless sort of man, so I just figured he'd taken off and stiffed a bunch of people he owed money to. Never thought something bad had happened to him."

"Did he rent trailers often?" I asked.

"He rented a lot of things. Ditch Witch. Cement mixer. Grading blade for his tractor. But he did rent trailers on the regular. Usually it was the big flatbed ones when he needed to haul some equipment that wouldn't fit on a smaller one.

That last year he was renting big box trailers. Not sure what he was hauling with them. They came back pretty clean, and Buddy wasn't the sort to sweep something out before he returned it, so he wasn't hauling hay or feed or anything in them."

Stanley pulled a handful of folders out of the filing cabinet and brought them over to the table. He opened one and paged through the thin, hand-written, top-copy pages of the rental contracts. Lottie and I watched in silence as he searched. On the third folder, he looked up at us.

"Bingo." He slid the sheet over and Lottie and I both looked at it. It was a rental form for a six-by-twelve-foot box trailer. The form was dated June tenth with a pickup at six in the morning on June eleventh of last year.

"Here's the return." Stanley slid over some stapled papers.

On top was a return form showing that the trailer came back late on June twelfth. It calculated the extra amount due and was stamped paid.

"Wait. Buddy paid the extra day's rental?" Lottie asked. "On the twelfth when the trailer was returned?"

It didn't make sense. He'd paid for one day when he'd reserved the trailer. If Buddy paid for the extra day on the twelfth, that meant he was alive then. He'd been back in Reckless and alive the day after the hauling job and no one had seen him?

Stanley frowned, looking again in the folder. "Oh yeah. I remember that. There was an envelope with cash and Buddy's copy of the rental agreement shoved through the drop slot. It was weird because Buddy never paid his overages promptly. I always had to call him and hound him for months before he'd pay up. And cash? That was weird too. I asked John, my night watchman about it because the trailer was dropped off in the middle of the night."

"You have a night watchman?" I'd always assumed places like this just used security cameras and not actual employees.

"We've had some attempts at theft in the past and this equipment is pretty expensive," Stanley explained. "I've got cameras, but Brenda's got this younger brother who really needs money and refuses to take anything unless he feels he's worked for it. So he sits here in the office with the lights off and mostly sleeps at night, and I pay him. When I came in that morning and saw the envelope with the cash, I said something to him, and he told me about the trailer drop-off."

"Did he see Buddy?" Lottie asked. "Was it Buddy? Buddy's truck? Or some other truck?"

"Just hold on here and let me tell the story," Stanley scolded with a teasing smile. "My cameras are all pointing inside the yard, so they don't show the parking lot. That big diesel truck of Buddy's woke John up and he saw Buddy's truck and the trailer pull up. Man gets out and unhooks the trailer. Then he gets back in and John thinks he's going to leave. Instead he pulls up to the side of the office, hops out, shoves the envelope through the slot, then takes off. He was right in front of that big window there, and that's when John saw it wasn't Buddy after all, but Mike Allen."

Lottie and I both gasped.

"Are you sure?" I asked.

Stanley nodded. "John knows Buddy and he knows Mike. He flat out told me it was Mike driving Buddy's truck and returning the trailer. I didn't think anything about it. Figured that Buddy was doing some work for Mike and needed him to return the trailer. I know Mike doesn't have anything to haul that trailer with, so it makes sense he'd borrow Buddy's truck to do the return. And while Buddy might not be prompt at paying the overage, Mike's got a reputation for paying on time. The cash thing was still weird, but I wasn't gonna complain." He dug in the folder. "Look. I still got the envelope it came in."

"Don't touch it." I shot a hand out to stop Stanley from picking it up. "There might still be finger prints on it. Can you leave it in the folder along with these invoices? I'm going to text Jake and see if someone from the sheriff's department can come by to get them from you."

Stanley nodded. "Will do. You think this has something to do with Buddy getting killed?"

"Buddy went missing around that time," Lottie explained. "This might be important evidence in that case."

Stanley looked absolutely thrilled to be the one holding critical evidence. He carefully returned the paperwork to the folder and set it aside, vowing to not let it leave his sight until Deputy Sean or Jake arrived.

As Lottie and I were driving back to the campground, I texted all the information to Jake, making sure to tell him about the envelope that might still have fingerprints on it. His boat had remained docked in its slip again this morning for the third day in a row, so I knew he was still busy. Hopefully this information would help.

And hopefully he'd either have the case wrapped up by Saturday night, or be able to take a quick break, because I really wanted him to come along on my first sunset cruise.

CHAPTER 22

I eyed my phone for new texts and saw nothing.

"We're ready, Miss Sassy," Austin told me.

It was Saturday evening. Mom and my friends were on board the pontoon boat. Elvis was at the camp store with Flora. The coolers were on board with waters and bottles of champagne nestled in ice. The small sandwiches—a selection of ham, turkey, or cream cheese and veggie—were on a table along with the charcuterie tray, all covered with domed screens to keep the bugs out. Mom, Lottie, Sierra, and Danielle each held a plastic flute filled with bubbly. The sun had dipped low over the lake and we needed to set sail to be in the optimal sunset viewing spot at the right moment.

But I hesitated, because Jake wasn't here yet. He'd sent a positive RSVP to my text Friday night, but I hadn't heard anything from him since. He hadn't replied to my message about the trailer return, and he hadn't let me know that he needed to cancel.

Just as I was ready to tell Austin to head out, I saw Jake's truck pull into the parking lot. He sprang out of the vehicle and ran across the beach, not slowing until he'd reached the end of the dock where the pontoon boat was tied.

"Sorry," he panted. "It's been a crazy week. Wasn't sure I'd make it in time."

Jake leaned over to untie one side of the boat while I did the other. We both hopped into the boat. As Austin pulled us away from the dock, I went and got Jake and myself a glass of champagne.

"Here. You look exhausted." His clothes were rumbled. There were dark circles under his eyes. His beard was edging toward unkempt.

"Thanks. I *am* exhausted." He held the plastic flute out and tapped mine. "But we have cause to celebrate. You're launching your first sunset cruise, and we arrested Mike Allen today."

"What?" I exclaimed. "For murder, or for the electronics theft?"

"Murder." He grimaced. "The company didn't want to prosecute the theft. I went to them Wednesday morning with the GPS collar as well as the serial number on Joy Ann's phone. They confirmed the items had been stolen and launched an internal investigation. Other than confirming the theft, they pretty much shut me out, saying it was an internal matter. I didn't have enough evidence to get a warrant yet, so I went another route."

"Did Mike get fired, at least?" I asked.

Jake snorted. "Suddenly retired. Golden parachute and all."

Ooo, that made me mad. If Mike had been a warehouse worker or an order entry clerk, he would have been fired with no benefits, and probably been prosecuted by the company. It seemed like executives got away with everything —well, everything except murder, hopefully.

"I spent the rest of Wednesday making calls to some law

enforcement connections in the Richmond area, and managed to get a lead on the reseller. I pulled in some favors and a detective buddy brought the suspected reseller in for questioning. He denied knowing any of the items were stolen, but positively identified Buddy as their delivery guy. Last delivery from him was June eleventh of last year. The detective pushed the guy hard, but he doesn't seem to have any knowledge of Mike."

"Mike had to have arranged for the sale of the stolen goods somehow." I frowned. "Unless Buddy did it. But did Buddy have those sorts of connections?"

"He might have. Or Mike might have been dealing with someone higher up the food chain than this reseller," Jake said.

"So you had Buddy solidly connected to a theft ring through Mike's company," I confirmed. "And it sounds like Rio Grande found out Mike was part of it, although you didn't have that evidence from the company."

"We didn't, and I wasn't sure we had enough connecting the theft ring to Mike to go before a judge. But finding the truck changed everything," Jake explained. "That job site was locked, and Tony said there had never been any break-ins. That meant someone let Mike in so he could ditch the car. Tony made a few calls, and one of his employees admitted to lending Mike Allen his keys to the gates early last June—June twelfth, to be precise. The guy said Mike approached him and said he wanted to go in and see that cliff one last time before it was razed. The employee knew lots of locals were sentimental about that spot and didn't see anything wrong with it, so he loaned Mike the keys. Mike returned them the next day. The employee remembered the date because it was his wife's birthday and he was a little late taking her to dinner since he had to run the keys over to Mike."

I frowned. "But no one saw him arrive with the truck or

drive it off the cliff, did they? Mike could just claim that he went out there for old time's sake and that someone else, like an employee with a key, was the one who ditched the truck."

"Yes, but John, the security guard at the rental place, seeing Mike driving Buddy's truck and returning the trailer on the twelfth helps tie it all together. Buddy rented the trailer on the eleventh. Was seen in Richmond delivering to the reseller the afternoon of the eleventh. Mike was seen with Buddy's truck and trailer on the twelfth, and asked for access to the construction site on the twelfth—the same site where Buddy's truck was found. It gave us enough cause to bring Mike in for questioning, to ask him what he was doing at the job site on the twelfth, and why he was driving Buddy's truck and returning the trailer on that same night."

"So you took him in for questioning?" This was all so fascinating, that I had completely forgotten about the sunset cruise.

"Yep. But before we brought him in, Sean managed to get a warrant for Mike's banking information and cell phone records. Buddy's stolen electronics being connected to Rio Grande, plus the truck, plus the trailer return gave us enough for a judge to sign off on it. We found lots of calls to Buddy's phone and from Buddy's phone to Mike up until the night of the eleventh. After that, there was no more communication between them. We also found large unexplained deposits of cash into Mike's account. Buddy had a reason for large cash deposits given his businesses, but Mike didn't. It all gave us enough to bring Mike in for questioning and to eventually charge him with Buddy's murder."

I eyed him. "Is that going to be enough? I'm assuming Mike didn't confess."

"No, he didn't. He claimed he was returning the trailer as a favor to Buddy, and using his truck because he didn't have a vehicle to tow it. Claims he never saw Buddy after he returned the truck and that he was at the cliff to reminisce. Once we brought out the deposits and the call records, he lawyered up." Jake shrugged. "It's a whole lot of circumstantial evidence, but all together with the timeline, it's pretty convincing. I think he'll serve time, whether that's on a plea deal or through a trial, I don't know, but I don't think he'll get away with it."

Hopefully they'd find something more in Mike's house, or someone would come forward who had additional evidence, because I really didn't want that man to get away with murder.

"Sassy! Jake! Come watch." Mom waved us to the front of the pontoon boat where everyone crowded, champagne flutes in hand.

The sun touched the edge of the lake, gold and red reflected in the water, the sky lavender with pink-tinged clouds. We all stood in silence and watched as the glowing orb sank lower and lower on the horizon until all that remained was the faint glow in the sky.

Everyone cheered and clinked their plastic glasses. Austin turned the strings of lights on and slowly turned the boat around. We ate, chatted, and drank until the boat was safely docked and tied off. As I watched my friends leave, I felt joy bloom up inside me. It had been a beautiful evening. I knew my guests would love these cruises, as well as the history and ghost tours. And I'd love them too.

A murderer had been arrested. A victim would have his justice. And me? I had friends, family, and a business I absolutely loved.

* * *

A NEIGHBORLY STABBING, book 5 in the Reckless Camper Cozy Mystery Series, will be out in 2023!

Can't wait that long? Try my other books in the Locust Point Mystery Series, starting with The Tell All.

Never miss a new release or a sale. Sign up for my newsletter and get all the fun with none of the spam.

ACKNOWLEDGMENTS

Special thanks to Lyndsey Lewellen for cover design and Kimberly Cannon for editing.

In memory of my mother who was my biggest fan and my partner-in-crime.

ABOUT THE AUTHOR

Libby Howard lives in a little house in the woods with her sons and two exuberant bloodhounds. She occasionally knits, occasionally bakes, and occasionally manages to do a load of laundry. Most of her writing is done in a bar where she can combine work with people-watching, a decent micro-brew, and a plate of Old Bay wings.

For more information:
libbyhowardbooks.com/

ALSO BY LIBBY HOWARD

Locust Point Mystery Series:

The Tell All

Junkyard Man

Antique Secrets

Hometown Hero

A Literary Scandal

Root of All Evil

A Grave Situation

Last Supper

A Midnight Clear

Fire and Ice

Best In Breed

Cold Waters

Five for a Dollar

Lonely Hearts - coming in 2022

Reckless Camper Mystery Series -

The Handyman Homicide

Death is on the Menu

The Green Rush

Elvis Finds a Bone

Lightning Source UK Ltd.
Milton Keynes UK
UKHW011518230223
417527UK00001B/67